The Island

Frankie Rowland

Contents

IH E

C HAPTER 1

Any second now. In just a moment the clock would strike 12:00pm, and Russia would wonder why it was that he wasn't able to get out of bed again.

Just wait. It'll only take a second. It's bound to chime eventually. How slow did time move again? Russia couldn't decide if his clock was broken or if time had slowed. It seemed like a lifetime ago he was actually up and out of bed.

Lately he hadn't been trying very hard. Yet he wasn't sure why he felt this way. He had always been gloomy sure, but never to such an extent that he spent the better half of two weeks in bed.

He wanted to get up, he really did, but he couldn't see a reason to. Beyond his bed covers was a waking nightmare. He wasn't able to brush his teeth, cook his own meals, brush his hair, shower or even dress himself. Beyond his bed was him; a living disappointment so useless he couldn't complete even the most menial of tasks.

And Russia didn't want to spend his days being him. So he stayed in bed where it was safe and warm. Where even for just a moment, he was at peace.

Ah, there it is. The mechanical chime of his alarm, reminding him pitifully that he was being lazy again. He had to get up, it was impossible to ignore the terrible smell he excreted, and how roughly his stomach rumbled. He needed to get up, even his clock told him so.

Yet he couldn't. He was too fatigued, too sick. His head was still pounding from his hangover and he felt his heart weighing him down. The Russian groaned, and with a hand balled in a fist, punched the top of his alarm clock to stop it.

He would get up later. It's not like he had any plans that day anyway. He didn't like to make plans anymore, because he knew by the time they came, he wouldn't want to go anymore.

He hadn't even gone to work in the two weeks he had been feeling morose. Yet no one thought to check on him. He hadn't received a single text, call or a knock on his door. They had left him to die alone, and he was surprisingly okay with that.

This is all his life is after all. Staying in bed until his growling stomach forced him up and to the kitchen. He would then eat stale food alone, before downing it all with alcohol, and forgetting his problems.

It was hard to continue like this. He wouldn't openly admit he was lonely, but he knew a friend would do him no harm. Yet it never seemed as though anyone wanted to be his friend. No one really liked him. He felt so alone.

Maybe today was the day he was to fall? To give in, to set himself free. Maybe, this was the day he so longed for.

Russia rubbed his eyes. Then opened them. His bland wooden ceiling greeted him. If only he woke up somewhere else, he wasn't sure he could keep up with much more of this.

He had always hated that wood anyway. It was too loud, and it was too cold. He wished he lived somewhere else, somewhere far away from here, far away from himself.

Yet alas how could he complain? He had everything he had always wanted. But he still couldn't get out of bed. There was no reason to, there was no reason to do anything.

Russia sighed, what a stupid thing to think. Why couldn't he think of something smart for once? Why did he have to be so unbelievably stupid?

There was another meeting again today. It was supposed to be an antiwar consultation to ward off the growing tension between the countries, and yet Russia couldn't even bring himself to show up for it. He hadn't gone to the last one, or the one before that, he hadn't left his home in two weeks, but still no one seemed to worry.

He was required by law to go. But he didn't care. It didn't matter, nothing matters. If war was what they wanted, it was none of his business to tell them no. He couldn't even remember who was having tension, everything just felt like such a blur.

A buzz sounded through the empty room. Russia turned his head to look at his phone. Someone finally texted him.

He would have looked at the message, part of him really wanted to, but he couldn't bring himself to. What if it was bad news? What if it was UN or America messaging him to tell him how much of an asshole he was being?

It didn't matter anyway. Russia never really looked at his phone anymore. It held too many memories, too many people could check on him through it. And that was the last thing he wanted.

Russia sighed, then looked back at his clock. 12:05. Its amazing how slow time passes. He should really be up by now, his stomach was demanding some food.

Come on. This shouldn't be this hard, he was just being a stupid piece of shit. If America could do this, so could he. Russia huffed, then pushed his duvet back and sat up.

Immediately he was hit by the cold air of his unheated cabin. He would have put the heating on if it wasn't for the fact he had passed out before he even had the chance to have dinner.

With a chest too tight to breathe through, Russia tossed his legs over his mattress.

The Russian looked around his room. It was a mess. There were clothes and plates everywhere, bottles of vodka strewn around the room in a pitiful display of his lack of self control.

This house was a nightmare, he already wanted to go back to sleep.

Slowly, Russia stood to his feet. His head still reeling from his hangover, his heart still heavy from crying. Well its now or never.

The Russian shivered was he left his room. He really aught to put on the heating. He'll do it later... maybe. But for now Russia just tumbled down the corridor, and to the kitchen.

The smell that hit him once he arrived reminded him that he hadn't gone shopping in a while. Most things had gone off, but he couldn't have been bothered to throw them out. He always felt more tired after eating, so he usually went back to bed, leaving him no time to do anything.

He grabbed some stale bread, which was so hard he couldn't even spread butter over it. But that was fine, he hated butter anyway, and he never enjoyed bread that much to begin with. It was just like everything else, a let down.

Dragging himself to his fridge he pulled out some ham. Though it hadn't escaped him how empty his fridge was, he barely even had any milk left, and even then he wouldn't have been surprised if it was spoiled. He aught to go shopping soon.

Leaving the fridge he went back and finished his sandwich. There was nothing to it and the ham smelled funny, but it was the best he could muster up.

The Russian country sat down at his counter then took one bite, and felt his eyes swell up. How did everything get so difficult for him? Why was it him of all countries that was so lonely? Why couldn't he be like everyone else?

Russia sighed, and gazed around his kitchen. Trying to keep himself away from his thoughts.

He hated to listen to them, they always said the same things. But it never hurt any less. He could hear them now, pulling away at his heart and robbing him of his energy.

'I hate what I've done.'

That voice whispered in the back of his mind. Even as he took the last bite of his stale sandwich, he could hear it cry out for him. How could he live like this?

'I hate my life.'

It repeated. Nagging the flesh of his mind until he was so fatigued he felt like falling asleep again. The world seemed so far away, why did he get up again? Nothing good came from this, he should go back to bed, he's done enough today.

'I hate mornings.'

It continued even as Russia stood up, leaving his dirty plate, and traipsed into his sitting room. His Siberian husky; Toska, wagged her tail as soon as she saw him. He had better feed her, she deserved better than this.

'I hate waking up.'

He heard it cry as he retrieved some dog food for his beloved. His head was spinning again, he better hurry back to bed, he couldn't take much more of this.

'I hate these walls.'

He listened to it as he gently caressed Toska behind her ears as she ate, tail wagging. He felt nothing but envy at her oblivious joy. Oh if he could live like her, no stress, no sadness, no hatred, just ignorant bliss.

'I hate this room.'

It muttered sadly while he walked back down the hall, he saw himself. A long mirror stretched through a dresser, and gave him a view of himself. Oh god. He looked disgusting.

'I hate this house.'

That voice whispered as he looked himself over. He had been wearing the same clothes for those two weeks. Grey socks, a blue long sleeved shirt, black basketball shorts. He didn't even put his ushanka on, his hair was too greasy to wear over it, he found it made him feel even grosser.

'I hate myself.'

It told him as he stared at his sunken eyes and frowning face. His hair hadn't been brushed in weeks, he hadn't showered and he hadn't brushed his teeth, he was a disgrace. This wasn't the expression of someone who was happy. And everyone could see. It was just what he wanted them not to, so the Russian begrudgingly turned away, and dragged his feet back toward his bedroom.

'I hate everything.'

It sobbed as Russia-

A knock came at the door.

It was loud and precise, calculated to warn him. Russia froze, and slowly turned himself around. Finally, it had only taken two weeks for someone to come check on him. Should he be feeling honoured? Surely that was a high score.

The Russian country stepped back down the corridor, and peeped around the corner to the wooden door.

A shadow blocked the light from under the door. Someone was definitely out there. Oh if only he had checked his phone, perhaps the person at the door was the one who had texted him, then maybe he wouldn't be feeling so anxious right now.

Russia walked forwards and stood before the door, his hand on the handle. 'Just open it,' he thought, 'whats the worse that could happen?'

Yet he continued to stand there like a deer in headlights. Why was this so difficult? Why was he so difficult? He couldn't open it, he looked like shit, he smelled like shit, his house was a mess, he was a mess, he couldn't do it-

"I know you're in there Russia. Please open the door, I only want to speak with you." A familiar voice called from the other side of the door.

Russia felt his blood run cold. He would recognise that voice from anywhere. That angelically deep tone with no discernible accent.

Oh god. He had doomed himself.

T S O I

C HAPTER 2

"So vould you like some vater or uh, vodka?"

The man shook his head, his eyes ogling at the many dirty dishes and spilled food. His posture was stiff, as though if he were to relax, he would somehow end up with stains on his blue waistcoat. "You wouldn't happen to have any tea would you? It is awfully cold in this area." The man asked as he finally met Russias gaze.

Though Russia broke it almost instantaneously. He couldn't bare to look at his clean, glowing face. It was too much to handle when he knew he was disgusting in comparison. "If it's not a problem of course." The visitor reiterated, waving his hand almost as if to dismiss his first request.

Russia nodded, then turned away to retrieve a teabag, mug and to put the kettle on. He had never really liked tea, though he had tried many times to enjoy it. His pathetic attempts were the only reason he actually had teabags, he never really knew why he didn't just throw them out. But he didn't, guess he was lucky to actually have some.

"So Russia. You missed the meeting again today. Would you like to talk about your absence?" The man asked, his head tilted to watch as Russia placed the kettle on its holster, before switching it on.

The Russian physically winced. He was afraid to be asked that. Truth be told he had no reason for his behaviour, for his forced misery. He was just inexplicably sad, and he couldn't figure out why.

Russia breathed in, then open his lips to answer, his back still to the man. "Vell I-"

"Are you okay?"

Russia froze. Whatever it was he had been about to say had been lost. He hadn't been expecting that, he was waiting to be yelled at, called a piece of shit and then perhaps hit over the head. Then the man would leave with a threat to do much worse if he didn't show up again.

But alas. It seems as though he might never be right, he would always stay cursed to be wrong.

"Yeah," Russia breathed, "I'm fine." He could hear the man sigh, it was obvious he didn't believe Russia. But the Russian had no idea how to tell him the truth. There wasn't a single reason for his depression, it just existed in him. And he had no idea how it came to be, nor how to fight. He simply sat down, and let it happen. And he couldn't tell the man why he had done tha t.

"Are you sure?" The man asked again, this time more pressing. But Russia nodded his head slowly, "yeah, everything is fine." He muttered, his head low in shame.

Thats when the kettle popped, breaking the tense atmosphere with a strong shudder. The Russian country lifted his head, and reached out for the kettle, poured some water, and made the man tea. All the while neither of them spoke a word, which only made Russia feel all the more self conscious.

Hugging the mug between his hands, the Russian walked over to where the man sat, then placed the cup down in front of him, to which he quietly muttered a 'thank you.' Russia then sat himself down opposite his guest, his eyes drilling themselves into the counter.

"Now I think you know why I'm here." The man started before he took a sip of his tea. Opting Russia to glance at him for a split second before he looked back down. "However I need you to look at me while I speak to you."

Russia internationally grimaced. Oh god he messed up again. He was already annoying his visitor and he had only just arrived. With a heavy heart, Russia finally met the mans gaze and held it. Taking in his vitalised blue face overlapped by multiple white rings and a perfectly drawn map of the world. His ironed white shirt and tie, his pristine blue waistcoat, the white leaved halo around his well groomed blue hair. At long last he acknowledged the man's name, UN, United Nations.

"Sorry sir." Russia shamefully grumbled, his eyes darting back and forth between his companions eyes and the table. United Nations sighed, shaking his head subtly as though he were disappointed. Russia could guess he was, anyone would be. It had always bothered Russia how fast UN would resort to disappointment. No matter what it was the Russian did for him, it never seemed to be enough. Perhaps he just had high standards; which was one of the many things Russia was jealous about when it came to him.

"I have something serious to speak to you about," the organisation started, "I know you mustn't be feeling too great right now but that's no excuse for ignoring your work."

Russia blinked. His mind had been wandering again. What was it they were conversing about again? Something about him being a shitty person right? That would make sense, considering he was shittiest person in the world, and he knew United Nations thought that. He had to right? Wasn't that why he was here? To give him shit for not doing his job?

The Russian hung his head low, shaking it. 'Come on concentrate,' he told himself, 'be better than this.' Visceral shame burned into his cheeks and made his face heat up. His heart pulled harder against itself, by god he couldn't breath.

"Da, I know. I vas going to go to next meeting." Russia lied haphazardly, knowing full well he had no intentions of doing any of the sort.

The ever observant UN noticed this instantly, and shook his head with that same disappointment Russia so hated. "Look Russia. You clearly don't care for your responsibilities," the leader declared as he looked around the room, almost as if to point out the mess as some kind of proof, "so I've brought it upon myself to give you knew ones."

Russia felt taken aback for a second, perhaps because he was accused of not caring, or perhaps it was from the idea of 'new responsibilities.' Either way he suddenly felt rather baffled. "What does zat mean?" He asked as he crossed his arms and leaned back in his chair.

Uncomfortably however, after he had crossed them, he could feel the softness of his bandages under his sleeves. The tinge of unease brought upon him by the feeling forced him to unravel them, and leave them on the arms of the chair instead.

UN took another sip of his tea, then met the gaze of his beaten companion with shimmering eyes. Russia was always jealous of his eyes, they had always been so wide and alive. The kind of eyes that you knew could see everything. There wasn't even an outline of bags under them, they were as vitalised as they were observant. The world must be so clear through sights like those, and that idea made Russias jealousy flair.

The organisation spun his cup around in his hands. "It means that you're momentarily fired." He said, and took a sip of his tea.

The Russians eyes widened. Wait- what did he just say? God he needed to learn how to concentrate. "What-?? But I am kountry, you cyan't fire me!" Russia cried as he slammed his hands on the table, feeling his lassitude give way to vehement agitation.

UN scrunched his nose up. His eyebrows furrowed in disgust as he watched the Russian with narrowed eyes. "It'll only be for a year." He reassured his host. Though part of him knew he did little to comfort the country. UN would never formally admit it, but he knew that the country was drowning, and even if he tried to dive in and pull him afloat, he would be dragged down with him.

Even now as he stared at the man before him; face tight and old, a pitiful expression permanently stitched into his skin, an obvious adversity to taking care of himself. Even now, UN could see that he would never forgive himself for any of his actions, nor for simply being. He was a lost cause, and deep down the organisation knew that.

He watched as Russias sunken eyes flared irksomely, his hands balled in a fist. "How is zat giving me new responsibilities? You're just taking zem all avay!" The Slav yelled, his heart roaring in his ears, his anxiety nearly spilling over.

UN calmly ran his finger around the brim of his cup, slowly shutting his eyes in anguish. "If you would let me finish you would understand." He muttered gently, opening his eyes to be met with the horrified expression of his companion.

"I'm sending you to Ivymallow, Russia." The organisation explained slowly so the country could understand his every word. Yet Russia still pulled a disgusted face, his eyes narrowing suspiciously. "What hell is zat?" He spat.

"It's an island off the coast of Britain. I think being there for a while will do you some good." UN spoke lightly, trying his hardest to sugarcoat his words for his distressed host. Though it didn't seem to work as by the mere mention of Britain the Slav turned up his head, not unlike a child refusing to eat their vegetables, and banged his fist on the table.

"I'm not going to some island in Britain. I am kountry god damn it, you cyan't make me do shit." He bellowed. His haunted eyes fraught with a distress that was only known by people under an eviction notice.

The UN was surprised for a moment, no one had ever spoken to him like that before. He wasn't quite prepared for such harsh words. Yet he quickly slipped out of that, and acknowledged what the Russian had said. 'What a disrespectful little commie.' He thought as he narrowed his eyes and gripped his mug with taunt fingers.

United Nations lips pulled up in a snarl, his voice low and heavy. "Don't you ever speak to me like that Russia. I'm trying to help you, why can't you just behave for once in your life?"

Russias anger slipped from him. Was he really that bad? He had never seen UN particularly mad before, it wasn't in his character to have a wrathful inclination. Somehow, he managed to fuck up so bad he changed the normality of someone else's behaviour. God, why couldn't he do one thing right? How was it possible that one person could be such a pathetic mess up?

Russias lachrymose eyes slipped to the tables face, his head screaming at him, his heart barely beating, his chest cold. 'I should have just gone back to bed.' He told himself, wishing he could shut his eyes and wake up.

The organisation seemed to notice Russias renewal of his tangled woe-begone, and his face relaxed, his voice as sugar laced as before. "You'll be arriving there tomorrow."

UN glanced around the room. Piles of dirty dishes lay unwashed every-where; from the sink to the counter and island to the table. His eyes met back with the Russians."If you have anything left to do, do it today. There is no power on the island, and you'll have a job to do." He explained. A part of him hoped that Russia had noticed his eyes darting around the room so that he would take the hint and clean before he left.

But Russia was too hung up on a single word his guest had said to notice anything at all. "What is my job?" He asked, leaning his head forward and onto the backs of his hands, resting his elbows on the table. "You'll help operate the lighthouse." UN explained before he took the last sip of his tea.

The Slav tilted his head curiously. "I'll help operate lighthouse?" He asked as he watched his visitor swirl his cup around with his wrist, playing with the last drop of tea at the bottom. "Yes, theres already someone operating it but I reached out and she said she wouldn't mind taking you in."

Russia again felt baffled. So the UN was saying he was to quit the job he was born to do for a while so he could go be a roommate to some random woman in a lighthouse on an island off the coast of Britain? Was he mental? "I am not living vith some random girl in lighthouse just bekause you zink I am lazy."

Upon hearing his last few words the organisation dropped the mug gently on the table and looked Russia in his eyes. "I don't think you're lazy I just think you need a change of pace." He explained, hoping at least by a little bit that he was getting through to Russia on his little sales pitch.

Yet the country simply lifted his eyebrows as if to say 'thats some bullshit.' UN shook his head, why did Russia have to be so stubborn? Seems like he inherited more than his alcoholism from his father. "Look theres nothing to worry about. Toska will be taken care of and your home will be left vacant until you return," UN explained with a rough tone, trying his best to get through to the Slav, "I promise you there's nothing to worry about."

The organisations eyes suddenly softened, his lips pulled down in a small frown. "Russia you clearly aren't happy and you're not doing yourself any favours by sitting around and feeling sorry for yourself."

"I'm only trying to help you."

The Russians heart swelled. He hadn't expected him to say such a thing. He never thought his guest cared for him at all, their relationship always seemed so tense. Almost as though there was preemptively tension between the two at all times. Even the way UN looked at him seemed so evident to him that this was the case.

He could still remember the time United Nations looked him in the eyes and said "you never change for the better, you only ever get worse." He never forgot that moment, he couldn't forget that moment. Every word he thought of to describe himself as had been born from that sentence. The simple but irrefutable notion, that he would never change, that he would never get better.

UN continued, unknowing of how distant Russias thoughts had become. "I believe that living off-grid and having small responsibilities will do you a world of good." The organisation leaned himself on the table, gently tapping his fingers against the wood as he listened intently to Russias response. "But I don't even know who I'll be living vith! How is zat fair?"

UN reached a hand up to pinch the bridge of his nose. When he told EU this morning that he was going to visit Russia and tell him about his plan, the European Union laughed hysterically. 'I will sell my left kidney and give you all the money if he goes along with it without arguing.' UN hadn't thought much of it as he left, but now he could see that his friends point was right. There was no one quite as stubborn as the man in front of him.

"Look Russia. I really do think it'll do you some good, you really need to get out more and if you won't work then I suppose this is your best break." He pointed out, his fingers hitting one last beat before he stopped drumming them.

Russia deadpanned, his sunken eyes stared in the most unimpressed manner at his company. "Zats not what I said. I said I don't know who she is." UN stared for a moment, then leaned back in his chair and crossed his arms. "The lighthouse keeper?" He asked, more so to double check than to actually receive an honest answer.

Russia rolled his eyes. "Who else?" He jeered. "Watch the attitude," the organisation snapped before his face softened and he continued, "she's a lovely girl, I visited her not too long ago and she proved herself to be a very diligent young woman."

He could still picture the pretty lady he met at the docks when he first arrived at the island to finalise the arrangement. She had brought with her a bouquet of flowers picked from the gardens in her town and complied by the local florist. A small egg-white tag was wrapped around it, and in beautiful cursive the words 'from the people of Ivymallow' was written for him to see.

"I do hope you like them, the whole town pitched in to get you a little something." The woman smiled sweetly at him. By that time he believed she meant just the bouquet, and thanked her. However as he was brought on a tour around the island he was proven wrong. A little produce from everyone of all trades was given to him, much to his appreciation. Home-made beer, baked goods, fresh fruit, newly wielded knives, a hand crafted tie; the list went on.

As his hands slowly piled with a sweet welcoming he only came the more convinced that this was the perfect place for someone like Russia. And the lighthouse keeper was the most precious of them all; the star of Ivymallow. The young woman was warm and welcoming and had a kind air about her that drew those around her further in her orbit. "I believe the two of you will get along just fine." UN smiled quietly to himself. His eyes boring in his mug and to the black dotted remains of his teas excrement.

Russia eyed the gushing country weirdly. "Vell what's her name zen?" He asked with an obvious new intrigue. UN snapped his eyes up, the remnants of his grin still subtly visible upon his lips.

"(□/□)."

T L   P   W S

- -

C HAPTER 3

There was so little in this world that meant as much to you as did your pride.

Something beyond you was always pulling yourself back into your honour, your only trial of stability that made your world go round.

Yet once you received that faithful cursive letter, you realised your pride had to be put away, lest you drown in its murkiness.

That day was as ordinary as the last. You were at the post office for the newspaper when you were surprised to receive some post. Amy Rosalie, the woman who owned the post office was just as surprised as you were to receive a letter. Though it was its contents that surprised you the most.

Written in beautifully practised cursive was an apologetic question of whether or not it was okay for someone new to arrive. That part was shocking sure, but the name signed at the bottom shook you from the inside.

It was signed by the UN himself.

This was odd. UN obviously had much more important means to fret over than your tiny little island that had little over 20 people to call it home. Yet you didn't question much in the moment.

You merely rushed to call a town meeting and show the letter to every islander in your quaint town. Once the decision was clear, you hastily returned home to write an extensive reply on how honourable it would be to house a countryhuman.

You waited days for a reply, and once it came the town rejoiced at UN's recognition of them and the imminent arrival of the country UN informed you of. It would be Russia who was scheduled to arrive by the end of the week.

But time flew by as though it were a bird in flight. Today was the day he was to arrive. The whole town rushed to get itself together. The town square was decorated in lights and banners, bouquets of flowers bloomed from ribbons tying them to fenceposts.

The smell of freshly baked pastries wafted through the air, laughter was as loud as the asserted voices of demand.

The little kids ran to and fro, the elders sat to themselves waiting patiently, everyone with a fixed job was finalising the gifts they had put together for the country, and those without a job were finishing the decorations, tweaking and re-tweaking every little detail to assure everything was perfect.

Yet you tried to ignore all that. Today you were standing to the side, twisting and pulling on your hair, your feet shuffling awkwardly. You were a little more than nervous to meet the country.

What if you didn't get along? You wouldn't want to embarrass UN like that. This was your chance to put Ivymallow on the map, yet if it were to go wrong, you could drag its name in the mud.

You fiddled with your hair again, then looked down at your clothes and smoothed them out. "You look just fine (□/□). Don't worry too much, I'm sure you'll get along just fine." A gruff voice spoke from beside you.

Looking up, you notice Vivian standing beside you. His bushy beard overhanging his lips and blocking his smile from your view.

Vivian Dominic was one of your favourite people on the island. He was a thin old man who lived by the beach at the westside docks, he made a living by selling fishing equipment and caught only the best fish. Years of residing by the open sea air had left his skin thick with wrinkles and hair to grow wildly. Yet he always remembered to smile when given the chance.

"I know that," you stumble out, eyes leaving the old fisherman's and meeting the floor, "I just don't know what to expect."

Vivian smiled to himself, then gazed out to the horizon, half expecting the dreaded ship to sail into view. "Then don't expect anything at all. What's going to happen, will happen." His eyes slowly turned to meet your frowning face, his hand softly resting on your shoulder in a somewhat comforting manner. "Really theres nothing to worry about (□/□), it's possible you'll get along, but its also possible he'll be a total asshole, but that won't be your fault, it'll be his."

You laughed, ducking your head down so he wouldn't notice how worked up you were becoming. "Thanks Vivian, I appreciate that." The old fisherman smiled, his thick skin creasing in a way that made him look even friendlier. "Anything for a lovely lass like you."

Your eyes returned to the horizon. The ocean beyond was a Prussian blue, its deep depts swaying back and forwards with a tousled rock, lulling itself into a peaceful rhythm. The open air brought a gentle breeze that combated the beating sun perfectly, and with the fluffy white clouds floating through the Cobalt blue sky you could see the day would turn out fine.

Rain wasn't visible for miles and the breeze seemed content to stay calm. It was a nice day.

The perfect day to show just how beautiful your home was to an outsider, just as it had been when the UN arrived clutching the railing of Arnie's boat. "I don't suppose you have a lighter on you (□/□)?" Vivian asked from beside you, his hands burrowing through his pockets with an unlit pipe now in his mouth.

"Im afraid not Vivie, you'll have to ask Rosalind, she never has a shortage." You answer with a smile, somehow taking delight in how the old man huffed in mild defeat. "I'll ask later, you probably wouldn't want me pu-ffing away when your little boyfriend gets here." Vivian replied, a playful smirk resting under his unlit pipe.

You place a fist on your hip and jut it out as though you were mocking an annoyed mum. "He is not my boyfriend, sir, he's my consort I think you'll find." Vivian threw his head back in a hearty laugh, his dark eyes closing momentarily. "Oh I do apologise your majesty, I assumed it was just a fling."

You smile wholeheartedly, your anxiety quelling amidst the found banter. "You are humbly forgiven my good man." Vivian smiled at you once more, then turned his sights back to the ocean with a deep sigh. Whether or not he too was expecting the dreaded boat to just appear was beyond you however. Perhaps he was simply admiring the beautiful view, or he was wishing to be safely back at his home, instead of waiting like a sitting duck for his life to change with the arrival of one person.

You glanced nervously at the marvelling clock imbedded into the wall of the post office. It was noon, he would surely be here any moment now.

You took a deep breath in, and smoothed out your clothes once more. "Shall we be off then?" Vivian asked as he too noticed the dwindling time.

You nervously nodded your head, then breathed in once more, your chest shaking with anxiety. "It would be best." You say, then take off towards the east end docks.

Upon noticing that you had turned to leave, most of the other people standing around followed after, bouncing excitedly behind you. Words buzzing with exhilaration was heard behind you, however you took no notice of their meaning, you simply marched straight on, constantly glancing down at you clothes to assure yourself you looked presentable.

By the time you made it to the east docks, the boat driven by its owner, was fully in view. It was at that moment did you realise how woefully unprepared you felt. Had you cleaned your home? Did you finish the morning logging? Did you make both the beds? Did you have fresh food? You didn't have a gift for him, would he be offended if you didn't give him one?

Unlike the day UN came to visit, you were told by everyone to not give your new visitor a gift as giving up your home for him was a gift in its own right. But now you were second guessing yourself. You should have at least given him flowers, maybe even some bread, he must be hungry after such a long trip. Surely his energy must be empty after getting up early enough to fly directly from Moscow to London, then travel to the port in Hull and furthermore waiting to be shipped over to Ivymallow all before noon. He must be starving, ever the more thirsty. Perhaps a bottle of water would hav e sufficed as a gift as anything was better than nothing.

Yet here you stood, watching him approaching with nothing to show for yourself but being here. Maybe Vivian was wrong, perhaps you'd already ruined your first impression and skewed your chance of ever getting to know the country. Your heart reeled in your chest, your anxiety heaving.

You watched the boat approach with fingers of anticipation gripping you in every corner of your mind. Its blue body was wooden with light masked sails bringing it slowly forwards. From the small distance between the docks and the boat, you could recognise Arnie Louis, the man who brought people to and fro when deemed necessary. Yet you could also see a man behind him, someone you didn't recognise.

Just like when UN had come to visit, you found yourself marvelling at how different the man looked. He was tall, so tall it looked as though he were standing even when he was seated. His skin was red and his body leaned back against the rim of the ship.

Though it was hard to make it out, you knew it was Russia.

Your heart bet faster still. This was it, you couldn't run from your doing now.

T M s E   M

C HAPTER 4

"Hey."

Russia pulled his head up, his eyes meeting an older man standing in front of him, his hair white and his eyes overshadowed by dark sunglasses. "You're Soviets son right?" The man asked, his star spangled complexion catching the darkened sun, making him look as though he was much younger than he was.

Russia didn't reply, he simply stood and stared at his fathers new found ally. "Not much for talking huh?" The man asked with a smile on his white lips. Russia wasn't even sure why this man was speaking to him, he was only here because his father had given a vague excuse. Perhaps he wished to look more presentable by having a young child with him, as Russia was only 9, or perhaps he simply wanted him to be connected to other countries at a young age.

The Russian knew little of this conference his father was at, however he knew he was safely within the Soviet occupation zone, which meant he didn't have to be worried about seeing western ideals play out. He had been told they were in Potsdam, but this meant little to the child, he didn't understand what this meeting was about nor why he was here. But he knew even less about why this foreign man was speaking with him, or trying to would be a better phrasing.

He recognised his flag, the one that his father had warned was a symbol for the dirty capitalist world, the filth of humanity; the fallen man. He was raised on the concept that the man before him was a devil in his own right, and that he must stay away from him. However the Russian couldn't understand why his father told him all that. He quite liked his glasses, they looked rather fun to wear and they made the man somehow look more approachable. Part of him wanted to ask to try them on, only for a second though, they were probably too big for his head.

"What's your name little guy?" The man asked, bending down so he was squatting to look the Russian child in the eyes. Russia pondered for a second, staring into the barred eyes of the man before him. "Russia." He answered in his childish high pitched voice, his rather noticeable lisp caus-ing his name to sound a little silly.

But the man just smiled, finding endearment in the child's subtle struggle. "Russia huh? That's a nice name." The man said as he stuck his hand out for the Russian to shake.

"My names (□/□)."

Russia blinked, as if it would shake off his potent déjà vu. He then took your hand in his, and shook it, though he couldn't help but admire your silky soft hands. God, his must feel like sandpaper in comparison. "It's nice to meet you (□/□), my name's Russia."

You smiled at the tall country. You found it rather cute that he told you his name instead of saying something like 'I'm sure you already know my name,' it was endearing of him to say the least. It was rather amazing to see him up close. He was tall, incredibly tall, perhaps over 8 feet. Although you could see he was rather handsome, it seemed to be rather hidden under his deep eye bags and the solemn expression he kept on. He wore a blue and white striped shirt under a puffy blue jacket, which he kept his hands tucked snuggly in. Atop his head was some kind of fur hat, grey in colour with a pop of red where he had a small star in the middle. "The pleasure is all mine Russia." You smiled, dropping your hand back to your side and straightening your back, praying to god that you looked at least somewhat presentable.

"Are you too jet-lagged to go for a walk?" You question, trying your best to ignore the insistent voice that cried about how you looked, trying its hardest to convince you that you were making a fool of yourself.

But the Russian didn't notice your uncomfortable stance, nor the way you constantly glanced nervously away from his eyes. He simply looked up and around him, steadily taking in the scenery and the crowd of people waiting on the land. "I should be fine, I had few breaks here and zere." Replied he, his eyes making their way back to you, his face settling into what seemed like his resting face; which unfortunately for him was a bitch face.

You muttered a simple okay, your fingers playing with themselves as you messed with your feet, knowing full well this interaction was awkward. "Well then lets go, best to get you settled right away so you feel right at home here." You then began walking backwards and gestured for him to follow, to which he does with his hands firmly in his blue jacket's pockets. "Thanks for giving him a lift Arnie!" You call to the old shipman, who looked up from fixing his boats rope to the hoister. He gave you a small salute with two fingers calling back a simple "you're welcome m'lady" before he turned back to making a knot.

You laugh quietly to yourself before you lead Russia away from the docks, and towards solid land, something you knew he must be craving right around now. "I know you're probably very tired from all that travelling but everyone is very excited to meet you." You tell the Russian, who looked down at you with his glared eyes. "Yeah zat's not problem, I don't mind."

You smiled as a response, trying your upmost hardest to dissolve the ever present knowledge that all of this was painstakingly awkward. Yet you hoped beyond all thoughts that having the other islanders swarming him would take your mind off of it. Perhaps thats why you let it happen, why you stood back as you hopped up the steps and brought the country to the group of people awaiting his presence.

Immediately upon stepping up the last concrete step, you melted into the crowd, and smiled widely as each person you know rushed forth and held out their offerings to him. Russia seemed surprised at first, one of his hands flew out his pocket as he brought it against his chest, almost like a defense. Everyone began speaking at once, and you only heard snippets of their enthusiastic words. It wasn't long until Russias hands were full with gifts and offerings, each one balanced precariously in his arms.

He held flowers, a bottle of fresh milk, a carton of fresh strawberries, a handmade black tie, a bottle of imported Russian vodka, a small box of donuts- the list went on. Though your favourite by far was the pink and red flower crown sitting cutely atop his fur hat. A little girl named Maya had spent all morning making the perfect flower crown for him, ruining Sarah Kacey's perfect flower patch in the process.

Even though you found it rather funny, you couldn't help but notice that Russia did not. He stood haphazardly with an expression that said at any given moment he would make a break for it. But you seemed to be the only one to notice his look of overwhelmed panic, the others seemed intent to ask him random questions that seemed to be bugging them. Tossing the mans feelings to the side entirely.

"You're so big young man, what are parents feeding their kids these days?"
Harper Connie asked Russia, her aged voice sounding frail yet joyous, her
amazement evident. In all her 86 years of living, she'd obviously never seen
a countryhuman face to face, though in fairness, none of you had, it wasn't
every day one of them just shows up at your doorstep.

"Uh well-" "Aren't you the one that married America?" A little girls voice
asked excitedly, her wide eyes staring at him with wonder from her place
latched to his leg. "I'm not-" "Maya! Leave the man alone." Maya's mother,
Marla chimed in as she attempted to drag her daughter off Russia by her
arm. "I'm so sorry about her, she gets excited around new people." Marla
gushed to the Russian as she pulled the little girl behind her, trying to keep
her from latching onto him again. "Oh it's okay-" "What's Moscow like?"
Josh Harriet yelled out from the back of the crowd, causing a few people
to yell in agreement.

No one here had really been off the island before, it wasn't something they
desired. Everything you ever needed in life was right here, there was no need
for anything more. But that tinge of curiosity into the wider world would
always remain, and though no one here would ever see Moscow, they still
wished to hear about it.

"Well it's-" "Is it true that you quit your job?" Thomas Harriet almost jeered
aggressively from the back, setting off a few curious 'what''s from people
around the crowd. This seemed to be the straw that broke the camels back,
and Russia finally stopped trying to get a word in, his eyes wide in an
expression that seemed to signal that those few words hurt him.

It was only at that moment that you decided to step in, and push through
the people standing in front of you. "Well it's been lovely guys but I think
I better bring Russia to his new home to get him settled down. He's still
exhausted from all his hours of travelling." You shout over the obsolete
whispers being hushed ear by ear. The Russian brought his head down to

face you as you began pushing him on his back to get him away from the crowd of people.

There were a few protests as the two of you walked away, but you don't turn back to address them. You really did want the country to feel comfortable here, and you wouldn't want that comfort to be thwarted by an angsty teen who thought it funny to question him about the work he had only just left behind.

"Zanks by vay." Russia muttered with his head bowed, fingers clutching the many objects in his hands. "Its no problem." You replied, your lips pulled up just slightly, your eyes on the ground. "I could see you looked pretty uncomfortable."

The Russian breathed in deeply, you heard his breath entering him and watched his chest expand before he expelled it. "Yeah I'm not good with crowds." He stated, his head turning away to look off the cliff side, down onto the rugged sea below.

"Neither am I." You reply, moving your hands to smooth out your clothes again, messing with each fold of the fabric. The Russian grunted, then said no more. He seemed content to simply examine his new home, choosing not to distract himself from the many views around him. Perhaps he liked the ocean, maybe that's why he stared at its blue waves as the two of you walked by, slowly approaching the white and red lighthouse you called h ome.

It had been a hard thing, to prepare for his visit. Everyone pitched in to help clean up the town, but it was you alone who had to piece your home together in such a way that would accommodate for his stay. This included dragging a second bed up the spiral staircase so he would have his own. But once all was completed, you knew it would find its worth in gold. After all was finished, and he was sent away, you hoped to god that he would leave a happy man. Perhaps even on a cold lonely day he would think on your little island, and wonder what became of it. But maybe that's wishful thinking, maybe you were thinking too far ahead. Somethings take time, and you wished not to rush into this head first.

Russia looked forwards again, and you noticed his jaw drop as he saw your lighthouse up close. It had a beautiful outside façade, with its red and white spiral stripes. But the inside was even more beautiful, as though it was cut right from a Wes Anderson film.

"Well here we are!" You exclaim, gesturing to your home, "I hope you like it!" You clamber forward, desperate to unlock your door and welcome him in, not wanting to make things anticlimactic.

You turn your head and smile once again at him before you threw the door open and bowed subtly, one arm welcoming him to walk in first. The Russian glanced at you, then lifted his head to catch a glimpse of the lantern room miles above him before he stared through the open door. The country then walked forwards, bending over slightly to get through the door way.

You walked in after, feeling yourself getting more and more excited to show him your precious lighthouse by the second. Russia stood in the middle of the round room, his neck craned to stare at the top above him. The ground floor was nothing more than the entrance way, it had no furniture other than the wooden spiral staircase that lead to the rest of the rooms.

You brush past the Russian and begin traipsing up the wooden steps, listening as Russia followed suit, your hand trailing up the railing as you watched his mouth fall agape in amazement. You giggled to yourself at the sight as you climbed up into the next room. Next to the staircase was a dresser filled with barrels and supplies, it was quite like a pantry only it was all stored behind the wooden doors of the cupboards.

You decide to not show him this room as it was virtually nothing and continued walking. The staircase only spun around the left side of the room, and even then it was compact with short steps, so each room still had ample amounts of space.

You ascended into the next floor. A small black fire powered stove lay on the left wall, a red kettle seated atop its unlit surface. With a little space to fit two chairs facing each other, a small wooden table stood near the right wall. Between the two lay a small square window, which filtered in meagre amounts of light, bathing the mint painted walls in a golden ray, the shadows looked so much more surreal looped between the lambency.

"This is the kitchen." You stated as you lifted a hand to show him. The Russian glanced around the room, perhaps noting the lack of decorations that would otherwise make the room feel dull, but thanks to the mint paintwork, it always felt somewhat homely. You then continue up to the next floor, hearing the Russian follow suit with clumping steps.

The next room was yours, the one the two of you were to share for the time being. Like every other room in your lighthouse, the walls were mint with a small square window cut into the left wall. Closest to the aperture was the bed you had brought up for Russia, you figured he would like to be closest to the window as it would allow him a nice view of the screaming waves beyond the cliffs edge. Against the adjacent wall was your bed. They were old things, thin metal frames with white padded duvets and linen, stitched together in floral arrangements. Beside both beds was a bedside table, atop of which sat gas lamps as you had no electricity, no one on the island did.

There were a few shelves on the wall in front of you, all stacked with classic literature you had read and reread a million times. There was still a room above the bedroom, but you weren't too keen to show him it as it was your workspace for daily logging of passing ships and the weathers behaviour.

You stepped into the room and allowed Russia to follow after. Placing your arms akimbo you turn and watch the country stare around the crammed room.

"Well this is it! It's not much I know but its all I've got." You knew he wouldn't be impressed by your room, after all he had been raised behind the walls of Moscow. His world was a million miles from yours, everything you knew was obsolete to him, for he knew far better. He had seen mountaintops scraping the sky and oceans descending down as far as the earth's crust would allow. He had been around the world and back, his feet had walked miles through snow, fog, rain, pounding sun and freezing cold. He had been to the end of the world, and walked right back. Yet all you had seen was a little village in England and Ivymallow, the most amazing sight you'd ever behold was when the Christmas lights went up on the main land and you could see them flashing from across the water.

You lived a million miles apart, and it showed through as you stood crammed into your shared bedroom. He had experienced wanderlust, and you had stayed put your whole life.

"It's fine don't vorry about it." The Russian said gruffly as he dropped onto his bed, causing it to sink under him and groan. His knees were nearly to his chin and every time he moved the bed seemed to complain, as if it knew he was too big for it. You glance awkwardly away and turn to descend down the stairs, finding it best to start dinner. "Hey." His voice called from behind you.

You hum and spin your head around to look him in the eyes, your hand glued to the stairs railing, but Russia seemed too busy organising places to put all his gifts than to stop and look at you. "I never zanked you properly did I?" The Russian asked as he slipped the flower crown from his head, placing it on the lampshade over his gas lamp instead. "I can't remember." You answered, now fully turning your body to face him.

The country looked up, his resting bitch face somewhat gone and replaced by a tender relaxation. "Vell zank you zen, I vas vorried about all zis to tell you truth, but I see now I have nothing to vorry about, I zink I might actually like it here." You felt taken aback momentarily, unsure of what to say. But in the end, you just smiled with a tilted head, your eyes glistening at the man before you. "I hope you do, you deserve to."

Though the Russian didn't smile back, he continued to watch you for a second more, before he looked away fully. You turned back to continue down the first few steps. From behind you, you could hear the country sit down, the squeak of his bed unmistakable. You couldn't help yourself but smile a little longer as you heard it. He truly was an endearing man.

T F I M

C HAPTER 5

The endless air screamed nothing. One world half awake, the other asleep as it turned adagio, feet planted and head down.

Where was he? Why was he here? He didn't want to remember the answers, though his mind carried the weight of knowing.

Part of him wanted to wake back in the desolation of his home. Safe from the prying eyes of people who thought he was admirable. What would it take to disappear? How could he leave this place? A world of desperate solitude surrounded him. He was isolated without a word to say in it. This was not his choice. How nice a world it would be, without him. An existence of man and beast not fractured by which he stood.

Russia lay awake, morning at his window, filtering in with a full smile. But he didn't care, nothing mattered to him. He couldn't bare to get up, this day was like the rest, nothing had changed. His heart was pushing down on him so hard he thought it would shatter his ribs. Maybe it would, at least then he would have a reason to be in pain. But alas, he didn't. He was blessed really, his position in life favoured many a fate that descended on those not so fortunate.

And yet he was throwing it all away, choosing to spend the day in bed, refusing to meet the waking world. How pathetic. How very pathetic.

Everyone else can do it, and yet he couldn't. He felt trapped within himself. As if his cloudy vision was a prison for his corporeal form, so unwilling to let him be as it choked him from the inside out. His deep Catoptric Tristesse gnawing at his mind every day. Keeping him locked in his home for every hour that passed.

The worst part about being here is that he was unable to hide. Everyone on this godforsaken island was so intrigued by him. Their interest delved deep and fascination prevalent. They were far in limerence, like he was some sort of gift for them.

To him at least, that was hurtful. Not because it was somehow objectifying. But because it was completely and utterly false. How could he ever believe someone thought he was amazing, when he hated everything about himself? If he could transcend this plane he would. But his legs had long since been glued down, and his mind stapled to the paper of air, denying him his freedom from pain.

Russia brought his hands up to cover his eyes. What time was it? How was he supposed to tell? He hadn't seen a clock when he first walked into the room. So how was he supposed to see one now that he was unable to see the difference between what was real, and what was not? His mind felt a million miles away, and he rubbed his dry eyes with a painful twitch. He realised he was losing himself further.

How could someone so meagre be such a waste of space?

It was absurd, it was fallacious.

The world would be better off without him. You would be better off without him. Oh, that's right. You. He hadn't understood at first, why the UN was so infatuated with you. And yet he saw it now. He saw it the first moment he laid eyes on you. You were such a sight for sore eyes he wondered what he did to deserve even seeing such a beauty.

He would get up, he should get up. But beyond his covers would be the very person that was on his mind. The difference between you and him was so prevalent it hurt to imagine being near you. Tainting your Elysian mind with his presence.

What would you say if you saw him like this? Lying awake in his bed. Hiding from everything that breathed. Protecting his life from the horrors of his mind.

Perhaps you would find it weird. Then attempt to get him up by telling him he was being a weirdo. Just laying there, breathing by a whisker and without a sound being uttered. Without reason, Russia brought a hand up and stared at his knuckles. His red skin a tad bit darker around his protruding bones.

His arm ached just holding it there. The light felt like it slashed past his skin, biting at his fingers like little midges. It was a strange sensation, but he didn't mind. The feeling was welcomed, it was always nice to be reminded that you felt anything at all.

Dropping his hand back onto his chest the Russian sighed. 'What are you doing?' A voice in his mind cried, 'Get up.' But he ignored that too. His mind knew it was best to get up, but his psyche said otherwise. Why get up when he knew if he were to, he would only sit around and do nothing with his day? That's what he never understood. Somehow, getting up and doing nothing was more productive than staying in bed and doing the same. At least if he stayed put he would be safe from the world beyond him, instead of being subjected to submersion.

How tangible a world we lived in. One that was able to make him feel like this. How lovely a thing it would be, to be like you. Uncaring about this perverted world. Uncaring about your own troubles and only living in the moment. Unaware, unbothered. Such a beautiful mind, such wonderful eunoia.

Man is a fool, there was no denying.

He was given life and threw it away for the complexness of death. He knew its consequences; yet came. Land after land was conquered and as he did so, he destroyed life. His own, and that of what came before. Man is a fool, and he was forced to play that role, he had not a say with words. He was what destroyed him; human. Though he had to admit. He envied those that were mortal.

Knowing that life doesn't end until the fall of his civilisation was a brutal construct. Even with death, he would awake again, unable to find peace until another came forth and brought him to his knees.

The curse of immortality was a fate he wouldn't wish upon his worst of enemies.

Even now, as he lay doing nought, he wished every breath was to be his last. Despite knowing he would never experience such a pleasure. Satisfaction was beyond his grasp, the love of life nothing more than a formality.

Why was it so hard to live? It was natural, and yet, it felt so irregular to him.

Simple pleasures were complex, and complexities a normality. Although he couldn't figure out why he was like this. There was a world somewhere out there, but he was the only one who couldn't find it.

Russia's eyes flew open. How long had he been thinking? It was frustrating that he couldn't know the time. But he had a guess that it was somewhere in the afternoon. Not because of the positioning of the sun, or a lucky guess however. But because he could hear the echoing stomps of footsteps clambering up the stairwell. Towards where he lay.

You were back.

He wasn't sure when you left, he couldn't remember seeing you go. He wasn't sure if he had been awake for it, or if he had been dreaming. But that didn't matter anymore. What mattered was the soft voice calling from the other side of the room. A soft yet confused voice, a tone he felt shame hearing as it was directed towards him.

"Why aren't you up yet?" You ask with a raised eyebrow. Feeling rather perplexed at the sight of the large country curled under his duvet that was held up to his eyes.

Russia didn't respond, he just groaned and pulled his covers higher. You stood and stared for a while longer, the Russian lying unmoving before he muttered, "I don't know."

You glanced around the room, looking for signs that he had been up at some point. But there was nothing. You sighed and brought your eyes back to him. He had turned his head to face away as though he couldn't bring himself to look at you. "That's okay, just get up soon. You don't wanna waste an entire day, it's so lovely outside."

Russia grunted and pulled his duvet higher. Rolling fully onto his side now, his back completely to you. "I don't want to," he complained through a hoarse tone, his throat sounding dry. You crossed your arms and shuffled with your feet. You had been hoping to get him out so everyone could see him again. They were all buzzing with excitement to get to know him.

To people like you; ordinary folk, his kind was both fascinating and spell-binding. To even see one in person seemed so chimeric. Almost like a dream formulated by a mind that had fallen too far into routine.

But you could see that wouldn't be the case. Huffing in exasperation, you step towards him. Russia didn't react to this, he seemed far too content to be left by his lonesome.

But you weren't.

He was a fool to think you would give up after some half-assed excuses that led nowhere. You stopped at the edge of his bed, now looking down over the Russian curled up like a burrito. "What?" He growled. An eye peaked to see what you were up to.

You turned your back to him in a reply. Then placed your hand down and threw your body back, landing on a narrow space on the bed. Between his body and the wall. Your legs over his and your arms folded neatly over your lap. Your head tilted to meet his eyes.

"What the hell are you doing?" The country snapped, his eyes now open wide and covers pulled back. "Uh keeping you company? What does it look like?" You snapped back. Although you were incapable of keeping a silly smile off your face.

Russia groaned, and dragged his covers up. Though to his dismay, he wasn't able to have them as high as he had them before. Your sitting body was holding the duvet in place, making it impossible for him to lift it any higher.

"What did I do to deserve this 6or?" He muttered to himself and pressed his face further into his pillow. Strands of hair fell down his forehead and covered his eyes from being seen. But you thought it was rather funny that he didn't have anything to cover the small smile pulling on the corners of his lips. "A boat trip mostly." You replied. Opting the Russian to snort at your words.

"If you want, we can stay here all day." You say slowly, hoping to ease him at least a little. "Yeah?" He asked, opening his eyes again. "Yeah." Meeting his gaze you made sure to smile, but he glanced away once he noticed that you were. "I'd like that." he muttered.

"So would-"

A knock came at the door. Echoing around the towering walls of your lighthouse.

You brought your eyes to face the wall in front of you. "Now who could that be?"

O H sD Es

C HAPTER 6

"One moment!" You called downstairs as another knock reverberated through the room.

You were descending the stairs as quick as you could, heels bashing against the bare wood. One last knock came at the door before you reached it. Then opened it.

For a second you were confused, no one was at the door. That was, until, you looked down. Coming face to face with the innocent eyes of two little children. One boy, one girl.

"Hello Miss, we came to see Russia!" The little girl squeaked, her body bouncing in excitement. Beside her, her male companion nodded enthusiastically, looking just about as ready to burst as she did. It took you a moment to fully comprehend what lay before you. As you stood opening and closing your mouth like a blubbering fish.

"Uh well, he's upstairs at the moment. So why don't you come back late-"
"But Miss, we walked all the way here just to see him, can't we stay for at

least five minutes?" The little girl gushed, her face fraught with disappoint-ment.

"We promise we won't be trouble." The boy said as the girl nodded wildly in agreement.

You turned around to catch a peak inside, wondering if Russia would appreciate the company or not. You had a feeling he wouldn't but thought it would be best for him to have at least a little. They were only kids and you really didn't want to hurt their feelings. You let a sigh escape your lips, then stepped aside. "Be my guest."

The kids wasted no time in shoving past you and clambering up the stairs, laughing at each other. You shook your head as you closed the door with a soft click, 'kids these days...'

You followed after them, simpering to yourself at the sounds of them laughing above you. They must be in the bedroom already, as you could hear a rather stressed-sounding Russia asking them where they came from.

Once you caught up and stood leaning against the stair's bannister. You couldn't help but giggle. Russia was holding the girl in front of him so he could look at her at eye level. His arms were completely outstretched, keeping her an arm's length away from him. Her feet kicked in mid-air as she giggled uncontrollably. The boy was at Russia's feet, staring up at his friend in amazement. You could imagine he was thinking about when it was his turn to be lifted.

But he was much more quiet than the girl was. So he stood politely at the country's feet, not saying a word but smiling widely.

"Russia," you called out, opting the country to turn and face you, "this is Maya and Aiden." Upon hearing her name being introduced, Maya waved at Russia and squeaked out a loud, 'hi!' The country winced at her volume, then placed her down. Turning to you he asked, "Are zese your kids?"

You shook your head, not bothering to explain to him that you didn't have any. "You met Maya yesterday, remember? She was the one who latched onto your leg." Russia seemed to think for a moment before the silence was broken by the girl's high voice. "Hey! You never answered my question."

Russia's nervous eyes flew to you as if he wanted you to tell him how to respond. But you just shrugged and walked around the bannister. Pushing yourself up to sit on it and watch what was about to unfold. Russia threw you a betrayed look.

"Didn't you marry America?" Maya questioned, her round eyes wide with excitement. Russia choked on air as he heard those words. Clearly not prepared for her to say anything of the sort. "Where did you hear zat? I don't even like zat pig."

Both Aiden and Maya's mouths fell open. Russia glanced desperately at you to do something. But you only winked at him, finding a keen enjoyment at how the kids humbled him so fast. "You can't say that, it's mean." Aiden chimed in, his head shaking like a disappointed dad. "Niet I didn't mean it like zat," Russia jumped with anguish, suddenly realising these were children he was speaking with. "I meant it as endearing term. He's pig bekause pigs are loveable and um... friendly?" Russia glanced at you once more. You shot him a cheesy thumbs-up.

"Oh well in that case I think you're a pig!" Maya effused, staring up at the country with wide sparkling eyes. You couldn't help but laugh at the Russian, who was now glowering at you from the corner of his eye. "Yeah vell, I zink zat voman over zere is pig as vell," Russia muttered more so to himself than Maya. But everyone in the room could hear. You stopped laughing and returned his glare before hopping off the bannister.

"Would you kids like something to drink, a bite to eat perhaps?" The two of them diverted their attention to you in a flash. In unison, they declared,

'Of course' and followed behind you into the kitchen. Fumbling over each other as they did so.

You could hear the heavy footsteps of Russia coming down as you waltzed to your fridge. Or what you called a fridge. All it was was a plastic-lined cabinet filled with ice to keep your cold foods well, cold. Reaching in you pulled out a carton of milk and set it on the counter. Going to the cupboard next that held the glasses. "Would you like something Russia?" You called out, drawing a 'niet' from the Russian country.

"Thomas said you got fired." Aiden suddenly spoke from his place at the table. Opting Maya to mutter, 'What does fired mean?' more so to herself than anyone else. You waited patiently for Russia's response, wondering what he would choose to say.

"Niet I vasn't fired, my post vas just moved." Replied a heavily accented voice. Though he seemed to hesitate as he spoke. Not entirely knowing himself if he was fired or not. As you reached into the pantry and pulled out a tin of biscuits you swear you heard Maya ask, 'What does post mean?' Though again, it was a question she seemed content to ponder rather than answer.

"Did you come here just to see Russia?" You asked them as you brought their milk and cookies to the table they were seated at. Maya nodded her head and hummed as she shoved her mouth instantly with a Custard Cream. "You've seen me, now you kan leave," Russia grumbled under his breath. You jabbed your elbow into him and muttered through gritted teeth, 'Be nice.'

Russia grasped his side and breathed a heavy breath in; scowling at you. But you paid no mind to him. "I'm rather surprised your parents let you walk all the way out here all by yourself. The cliffs are very dangerous this time of year."

That's when your heart dropped as you realised what exactly the kids had done. "Oh, our parents don't know we're here." Aiden giggled, catching Maya's eye mischievously.

You and Russia exchange a look, knowing now that these kids were not supposed to be here. You look back at them chugging milk like water and eating all their biscuits in one bite. Oh, their parents were going to be pissed at you once they hear about this.

"Well hurry up and finish then, I'll walk you back. It's too dangerous for you to be out there by yourselves." You sigh. In all honesty, you had been looking forwards to spending a quiet day indoors with your new roommate. You had already been out today and didn't feel like going out again. Especially since the walk to the town was quite a long one and you still had logging to do. But you knew getting Maya and Aiden safely to their parents was more important. You didn't want them to chew you out for being irresponsible.

Maya looked up in dismay. "Is Mr not coming?" She cried, dropping crumbs of her last cookie all over your floor. "I zink I'll stay here," Russia was quick to reply, shoving his hands in his pants pockets and leaning back. But Maya shot up from her seat in response and dashed forwards, straight for Russia.

"Oh please Mr, come with us," Maya begged, wrapping her arms around his leg. Russia threw a look at you that said 'SOS' before he realised he would get no excuse from you. He grunted, then rubbed his eyes with his index and thumb. "Fine, fine. I'll go."

Maya let go instantly, hopping on the spot a little before she rubbed her crumb-stained hands over her red dress. Once she was done defacing her mother's hard laundry work, she took Russia's hand. Then dragged him towards the stairwell. Russia stiffened, then looked back at you. He seemed unsure of what to do now. But you only smiled at him and gestured for him to go downstairs.

He turned away and allowed the small child to lead him towards the exit. Aiden stood up a little after, a biscuit still in his hand. Reaching up with his other hand, the boy held yours, allowing you to lead him away yourself.

You thought it was so funny how the disdainful Russian flipped on a dime as soon as Maya began gushing about random things. He didn't interrupt her, or say anything catty. He just walked beside her, listening intently. As though he had done it a million times.

Maybe sometimes, old habits die easy it seems.

T O O W K s

C HAPTER 7

"Oh God, I'm so sorry they were bothering you, I take my eyes off of Maya for one second and she's already dragging Aiden halfway across the island!"

You smiled at Marla, shaking your hands to dismiss her apology. "It's alright, they did no harm, really."

The wind whispered quietly around you. The Sun fell in shattered beams through the gathered clouds. After an eventful walk of listening to Maya pester Russia for a good twenty minutes, you had made it back to the town square— a large stone pavemented area lined with flower patches and flanked with three shops. Marla had been standing there talking quietly to Sarah Kacey, the mayor of your small town, when she had first noticed you approaching with her daughter.

"Well if they ever do it again, they won't be getting any dessert for the next few weeks." Marla declared sternly, looking at a sulking Maya who was staring in shame at her flat shoes. "I'll make sure they won't bother you too often. Especially now that you have a guest."

Your smile pulled down at your lips, you turned your head away. Russia was standing a few meters to the side, kicking the ground with his feet awkwardly. As if he knew the two of you were watching him.

"They didn't bother him much, did they?" She asked intuitively, making sure to speak low so Russia wouldn't hear, her eyes gazing at your turned face. "Not really. I'm not all that sure, he didn't seem to know what to do with them. But he didn't seem bothered."

Marla laughed, her voice bounding around the square with joyous energy. The sound seemed to make Russia tense up, flinching ever so slightly, before he let loose again. Continuing to kick at the ground, completely unsure of what to do with himself.

Marla's whispery voice cut back through the sudden silence. "How is he? Did he settle in alright?" You stared at him. His posture, his expression, his mannerisms— everything about him. He seemed nervous— awkward. As if he wasn't sure if this was where he was supposed to be. "I think so. I'm not entirely sure." You replied, prying your eyes off of him slowly.

"Give him some time, he must be having bad culture shock." Marla comforted the idea, smiling at you in encouragement. "But he will settle down eventually, just give him a bit of time."

Silence met the deadened voices. The breeze whisked through the late afternoon. Quietly, you turned back to face him once more, he was still repeating his actions, he still seemed anxious. Birds sang through the wind, the roar of the sea became clear, you could almost hear the buzz of the Sun peering down at you.

"Well, It's best I bring this one home and show Aiden back to his parents. It was lovely seeing you, dearie." Marla proclaimed with a smile, wrapping one of her arms around her daughter, drawing her forward. "Oh and it was lovely seeing you too Russia, I hope you enjoy this fine day here!" She called out, opting for Russia to finally draw his head up, though he seemed to struggle to meet her gaze. "Uh, Da, I vill." He answered, glancing away in nervous ticks.

"I'll see you around (□/□)." She said, then turned to leave, the two young kids following after her.

You stared at her retreating figure for a moment, then drew your head back to look at Russia. Upon noticing you looking at him, he broke eye contact, and darted his eyes everywhere but to you.

You smiled at his awkwardness, then walked over to him.

"Soooooo," you started, clapping your hands uncomfortably together. "What now?"

"I kouldn't kare less." He spat, meeting your eyes with a glare. You froze, then blinked. "Okay...? Well, how about we just talk...?" You asked, your voice quivering subtly, unsure of what exactly you should have said.

Russia scoffed loudly. "About what?" You thought for a moment, then intertwined your hands. "Um, do you have kids? You're really good with them." You asked with a marked hesitation, something Russia noticed. "Niet." He spluttered, turning away. You awkwardly did the same. "Oh."

The birds sang a little louder, the breeze brushed a little harder, the sea roared deeper from its cliffside prison, the waves crashed everywhere around you, the Sun met the ground with rejuvenated fingers.

You turned back to Russia.

"Hey, are you alright? UN had mentioned something was off with you, he said something about you being a little down, do you want to talk about it?"

Russia's face went pale, his white eyes widened until they stretched uncomfortably in their sockets, his whole body tensed painfully. His lips drew up in a snarl, the corner veins in his eyes popped and darkened, his head tilted up. "Zats none of your fucking business, how fucking dare you ask me zat." His voice exploded. Tone low and heavy, anger dripping off his words like water.

Your eyes widened, you took a step back. "I didn't mean—" But you couldn't finish your words. You just stared wide-eyed at him. "Zis whole zing is fucking stupid, zere's nothing wrong vith me, I don't need help. You're vaste of my time." He spat, then turned and retreated towards your lighthouse. His head down and steps quick. Leaving you standing there in shock.

It took you a moment to compose yourself. You looked around to ensure no one saw what happened. But there was no one around.

The birds sang a little lower, the breeze calmed down, the Sun slowly hid himself behind a flurry of clouds, the roaring sea became a white noise whining in the back of your mind. The day was wearing thin. And as you watched Russia's figure get smaller and smaller, the light around you seemed to follow him, the clouds growing thicker. You turned your head away.

Then the birds sang no more.

You dragged your feet towards the old rickety bench opposite the shops at the town square— just north of the hollowing cliffs that kept the sea at bay.

You sat down with a groan. Pushing your hands into your pocket you brought out a pack of cigarettes and your beautiful vintage silver lighter— a heirloom your Great-Grandfather once had with him during the first war.

Pulling a fag from the pack, you slipped it between your lips and lit it.

The only sound beyond the sea was the crisp burning of paper as the dim flame began to eat it away. You breathed it in, your anxiety flushing out of your body slowly, your beating heart calming.

You watched the waves from beyond the drop. The white foam the sea brought forth pushed onto the beach alcove miles below you. Though you couldn't see it. The cliffs reared too high for you to see the beach. The golden sands of shells were somewhere in the back of your imagination, your eyes could only see the blue waves soaring towards the alcove, breaking just before they vanished.

You looked higher. The skyline fell slowly, the sea drawing higher.

How sad were you now, to sit here on your own instead of chasing after him? He was obviously lying, of course, he was lying. There was something wrong, though how could you know, when he didn't even seem to know what it was himself?

There was no greater animosity than hatred for oneself. There was no contest. One cannot love another without first loving oneself.

You knew he didn't like who he was. It was obvious, inside and out, the way he treated people he interacted with, how he reacted to personal questions. It was nothing short of obvious acrimony.

But you truly did believe that under all that selfish hatred. The disdain for who he was as a person, there was a genuinely good being in him. And even though he didn't know it himself. You thought it to be true.

You took one last drag of your cigarette, then flicked it. The view of the waves vanished behind a cloud you expelled between open lips.

The waves broke, the cloud drifted, your eyes slackened.

Only if he knew there was.

T M s I G A O

C HAPTER 8

"I hate Russia."

You hated everything about him.

The way he only ever went out to drink— spending all the little allowance you gave him on liquor, or the way he was in bed before 5, and never out before 3. You hated that he had gotten your hopes up, with a promise of help and company, only to discover he was a miserable git with a passion for rude and snarky comments. You hated that he piled his dirty plates up on the counter for you to wash, or how he stole your cigarettes and always promised to repay you, then never did.

It had only been a week since you met him, and you already couldn't stand him— not in the slightest.

You had never met a man so full of himself, yet so useless. He never offered to help, and on the rare occasion you attempted to ask for it, he would say he would, then not act upon it. And once you reminded him, he would get angry, like a child being reminded to clean their room. He constantly talked down to you, as though he thought you to be gum on the soles of his shoes.

He made you feel like a mouse in glue and oil. Trapped for simply being alive, punished for being where you were, before he was, for being what he didn't like, nor want.

You were the mouse as he was the oil, this compromise the two of you agreed to, was the glue of it all. One was simply existing in the world it belonged in, the other was something introduced that meddled with the harmony of neutrality. But such differences needed a bridge, and whether it was intentional or not, that bridge too, hurt the little mouse. Everything was unfair to you, at least in your mind. Nothing was fair.

You couldn't lie. His words hurt— stung, even. When he called you names, when he put you down for asking him to do menial jobs, it burned in despair. But that sorrow— the heartbreak of great renown, it would sequester, then arise from within you, not as tears or panic, pain nor torment, but as anger. And as the week progressed and he sent you spiralling downward, you slowly arose back up. All that rage that was slowly boiling from his pettiness, it added up, and finally fizzled.

Though, you had to admit, the explosion was rather pathetic.

You hadn't yelled at him, you hadn't cried. You had instead, decided enough was enough, and marched to the one woman you always went to when you had problems; Harper Connie, an 86-year-old with a love of helping younger people and their relationships.

You showed up at her doorstep, nostrils flaring, face scrunched and fists clenched tight, with one single complaint.

"I hate him so much."

You knew, once you left her home, and returned to yours, you would find him in the same place you always did. On the floor of the kitchen, the back of his neck resting on the edge of the table, his legs and arms sprawled out in front of him, a bottle in his hands.

The light from the window behind him, just above the table, touched every part of the room, except for the shadow which Russia sat under— the shadow that engulfed him. You noticed it each time, how he sat in the most morose place he could have, his back to the world beyond, though he always made a point to look at you when you walked in. Those sad gleaming eyes burning into yours.

It was only then, in that moment— no other, did you resonate with him. Did you find the humanity to spare some appreciation for his existence. To associate yourself with him. Within his sadness, his disdain for the life he was given, you found yourself, partly at least. You recognised him in that moment, you recognised yourself. You saw the burning despair, the lonely suffering of worlds apart, the heartbreak as aching sorrow flooded him. You saw it all in him, just as he saw it in you.

Then, once you noticed the bottle in his hands, it all left you, and you hated him once more.

You breathe in a desperate pull of your cigarette, closing your eyes, pushing down the anger that was boiling inside of you again. "Well isn't that funny, I seem to remember you being so keen to have him before he got here, now look at you! My Dear, you've gotten yourself into a pickle." Harper laughed at your cross expression as she fiddled with her crochet flower.

You always appreciated Harper, for everything she was worth. You, naturally, appreciated her advice and ears, she was your go-to person when you needed to vent. But you always silently appreciated how young she was inside, and how beautiful she was outside. She had a heart of gold— the most resplendent woman you had ever seen. Her face was sunken with wrinkles that hung low on her skin, pulling her face downwards, but it never gave her a frown, if anything, it made her want to smile more. They made her pale skin appear soft and let the beauty of age trace every small detail of her dimples and edges.

She was exactly what you wanted to be when you were her age.

"I just don't know what to do! It's not like I can get away from him, I live with his sorry ass." You threw your arms up in defeat, then dropped them to the table, flicking the ash into a tray.

"Dearie, when a man is being difficult, all you have to do is give him a nice firm slap!" Harper implored, smiling brightly at you, showing off her pearly white dentures. "That'll show him his place."

You shook your head slowly as the old lady returned to her crochet. The beaded straps of her spectacles jangled subtly with every move her fingers made with her needles. "I just might at this point." You sighed.

"MISS!"

You jumped as the door suddenly swung open, revealing the grandchild of Harper, and the little devil that constantly hounded you about the man you wanted to forget about. "My mummy told me you were here, is Mr with you? I have some new questions for him!" Her high-pitched voice bled through the air, sending spikes through your temples. You hurried to snuff out your fag and push the tray away, acting as if it wasn't you who had caused the heavy stench of smoke in the house.

Harper smiled at you, watching as you stared wide-eyed into oblivion, your arms tightly crossed. "I hate kids." You muttered, drawing a pretty giggle from the older lady. Maya bounced up to your chair, leaning her little fingers against the legs and cheesing up at you. "Can I come to your lighthouse and see him, please please please?" She begged, her eyes wide and shimmering, much like a puppy's.

"Oh Lord, I am so sorry about her (□/□), that little divil still hasn't learned." A much more mature female voice came in from the doorway and as you heard it, you looked up to see Marla come in. She looked as disappointed as ever at her daughter, her head tilted as she gazed at her, her cheeks puffed out and lips turned inwards. Maya visibly shrunk under her mother's gaze.

"It's alright, I was leaving anyway." You smiled, dismissing her with a wave of your hand. You pushed your chair back and stood with your hands flat on the table. "Thanks for listening Harper, I'll come back some other time to catch you up."

Harper smiled her pretty smile, the many wrinkles around her eyes creasing a little more. "Ah it's not a problem at all Love, come back anytime you like, it's not like I have anything better to do!" She exclaimed, smiling ever the more wider as you walked past her.

"Oh and (□/□)!" She called, making you stop and turn back, catching a glimpse of the older woman turned in her chair, her crochet on the table. "Remember to give him a good slap!"

You smiled, she was the only person who knew how to make you smile like that— a real smile, full of joy.

Now you didn't feel so bad about being the mouse. It was something you couldn't control, so why fret?

T L   O O R

- -

C HAPTER 9

Breathe.

Remember what it is you're going to say.

You breathed out slowly, your forehead rested against the door to your lighthouse, your hand clutching the knob tightly.

By now the day was buried, the Sun digging its grave comfortably in the horizon. The first stars beginning to show themselves from behind a sheath of darkened colours. A chill hung in the air, gently caressing your hair, sending strands flowing across your shoulders.

Remember to breathe.

You opened the door slowly.

The hollowed-out comb of your house presented itself in the dark. The quietude of the echoing catacomb unnerved you as you stepped in, and shut the door behind you. It was somehow colder inside than it was outside and you found yourself pulling your body closer as you stalked toward the stairs, shivering. Did he not light the Stanley like you told him to?

Your anxiety emptied your anger, poking burning holes into your soul—draining you. Each step you took reverberated loudly around each and every inch of the room. Every small movement sounded like cracking thunder in the silence of the night around you, in the emptiness of the climbing walls you called home.

You couldn't hear him above you, you couldn't hear him shuffle or move, he was completely still. If he was even here at all. By the sound of silence, you were afraid he wasn't home. Was he at the pub? Or maybe he was in the outhouse. Or maybe, your anxiety was making you think silly things—excuses.

You swallowed a nervous lump, and continued up the stairs. Finally stopping at the kitchen.

And lo and behold, there he sat, just as you thought, with the back of his neck leaning against the table's length, his arms and legs sprawled out in front of him. Darkness ate him alive, the light from the window not even brushing against him, as if it refused to touch someone like him. As he noticed you standing there, he drew his head forward, so it hung limply toward you, his eyes staring up at you with that look you so hated, but so understood.

You didn't want to fall for it, he was asking for pity, it's what he wanted from you, wasn't it? If he had it from you, it meant he could have the power he once had, he could toy with you, take what he wanted from you— if he wanted anything at all that is.

You pulled your eyes from his, towards the basin instead. All the pity that could have been, now seemed so silly to you. He did pity him, but not for his misery, but for his utter stupidity.

Stacked in the basin were dirty plates, just like usual. He chose once again, to make you do the dirty menial jobs that he refused, like you were his personal maid.

Suddenly you didn't feel the pricking fingers of anxiety. You didn't pity his stupidity for believing you'd actually clean up after him. You didn't feel anything for him, not a single thing.

You weren't angry, you weren't disappointed, you weren't frustrated, you had no pity. You felt nothing at all for him. He wasn't worth your time to pity. You were above this nonsense.

With a small, careful step you approached him, his glaring eyes daring you to come closer.

You wanted to take Harper's advice, to scream at him, to belittle him the way he did you. But, with that one small step, you realised something, something you hadn't seen before.

And it made you pity him all over again.

It overwrote all the anger and resentment. You felt nothing but what you didn't want to feel for him.

In the overshadowed humdrum of the Sun's dying rays you could make out tear streaks down his face— his eyes red and puffy. Under his long-sleeved blue jumper were what looked like bandages— sticking just barely out at the cuffs.

He was staring at you with that same animosity he always held in your direction. But it didn't make you feel any less bad for him.

Maybe there was a reason he wasn't doing what you told him to. Maybe he was struggling to do them. You remembered UN had told you he was having a hard time, but you never imagined it may have been all that tough.

He was hand-fed everything from where he was from, at least in your mind. You couldn't imagine a world where he would be struggling harder than a working-class man.

But you saw now, through your pity, he was struggling in some other way.

You let your anger go completely. And smiled at him.

"Would you like to come see the city lights with me?" You asked, calling out into the darkness that shrouded him.

It was approaching Christmas, and as is customary, the lights had been installed along the quay on the mainland in celebration. You could see them so clearly from the town square at night. This day was when they were to turn on— first time in a year.

"Why?" Russia asked, his voice croaky and unused for quite some time— his antipathy still prevailing.

But you held your smile out, awaiting him to do the same. "I think you'd like them. They look beautiful every year."

Russia huffed. Turning to face the ground as if he was contemplating it— then relented. "Okay." He mumbled, then stood to his feet, stumbling a little under the numbness of his knees.

You turned away and bumbled back down the stairs. It felt much less hostile now you could hear someone else following with you. Your anxiety quelled completely.

Part of you was a little ashamed— not only that you let him off the hook again, giving in so easily after all the stress he caused you, but also that you had even been mad in the first place.

It wasn't his fault, you could see that now. If you had gotten angry at him, would that have pushed him further into despair? Or, whatever it was that was clearly bothering him so.

You didn't want to think about it.

You hated being the bother of someone else. You hated to think you could have ruined him just that little bit more.

You reached the entrance room and pushed open the door, holding it open from the outside so Russia could walk through. He didn't say anything as he did, and for a moment you internally groaned. The walk back to town was rather lengthy, you hated to think it would all have been in silence.

But as you began down the dirt road between the blades of grass alight in fiery fumes as the Sun settled its precious gaze downwards, Russia finally spoke first. "What's it really like living zere alone?"

You tilted your head upwards toward the Heavens. The horizon met the earth with palms outstretched, the yellows and oranges and reds bleeding across the sky as it fell downwards, and crawled back up. A breeze in the air. "It's lonely but I like it." You shrugged, letting your eyes relax as the clouds above turned pink like roses. "It would suck a lot more if the people here weren't so nice."

Russia looked down at you. "Vere you born here?"

You shook your head, meeting his eye. "No no, I moved here after I got the job."

Russia nodded, narrowing his eyes, as if he found your answer interesting. "How long have you been here?"

"Oh um." Your eyes met the ground, the narrow dirt path reached its muddied hands toward your ankles, your shoes flinging muck as you walked. "I wanna say three years?" You looked back up at him, talking unintentionally with your hands. "I got the job when I was eighteen."

Perhaps subconsciously, the Russian's eyes widened, as if he was surprised. "How old are you?"

You smiled, narrowing your eyes mockingly at him, playing with your hands in front of your body. "What's with all these questions? Don't you know it's rude to ask a lady her age?"

The sun fell lower behind you. The pallet of warmth at the ends of the earth before you washing into the blue seeping lower and lower towards the ground. "I'm just kurious, if I'm going to be here while ve might as vell get to know each other."

You exhaled a breath out your nose— quick and sudden. "You've been here a week and you still don't know anything about me?" The Russian shrugged, drawing his eyes to the blades of grass below. "I forgot to ask."

You felt your face heat up a little— embarrassment boiling your blood just barely. You had a hunch he hadn't forgotten to ask, but merely forgot his words instead. Ashamed of being seen in some way. Scared of hearing of other lives that differed from his own— the joy he just couldn't find. You felt pity for him all over again. You couldn't stop yourself from tearing your eyes away. "I'm twenty-one." You answered, only drawing a tiny, "Oh," from the Russian.

Then it went silent, just as you had been afraid of. The sun fell further. The hills beyond climbed the sky, stealing the light twisting in all colours from the gates of Heaven. The clouds drifted further, their pink tint turning blue as the night crept closer. Stars above your head twinkling as they awaited their cue for the Sun to rest and Moon to shine— the breeze turned colder.

Russia inhaled. Then stopped, his voice in his throat. You looked up at him, he returned your gaze, and spoke again. "Why lighthouse keeper zough? It's such odd job to have."

You shrugged. You hadn't really thought of that yourself. It was only that it was available at the time, and you had nowhere else to turn to. "Dunno, I saw it in the papers, applied, and just prayed I'd get it."

Russia kept his eyes on you all the while. Watching as you fiddled with your hands, fingers intertwined. "Do you like it?" You thought for a moment. It was a good question. For a while, you had hated it. Alone and isolated every moment of every day. Doing the same things over and over until you no longer felt human. Back then it felt less like a job, and more like a way of life. Your entire being built around this one little thing you chose on a whim. But then you got used to it— the monotony. Now, if you didn't have that stability every day, you thought you would lose your mind.

You simpered to yourself. "I do. It's a bit tedious but I like it." Russia seemed to notice how you reacted, and it interested him more. "What do you do?" He asked.

You looked back at the view. The evening was no more. True blue was everywhere around you, lights and darks meeting each other with hands outstretched, the stars having a moment to breathe to themselves. The town square was in view now, you could see the silhouettes of the buildings coming closer and closer. You counted off your jobs on your fingers. "Man the light, daily logging of the conditions, communicate with ships if need be, y'know, that kind of thing."

Russia hummed, his eyes meeting the town before him, his head nodding. "Sounds kool."

You laughed a little, glancing up at him again. "It's not, it would drive you mental."

You stepped onto the cobblestone square with loud thumps. Your footsteps bounding off the empty air around you.

You had a plan. Where you stood now, at the centre of the south part of the square, you would be able to see the lights just fine. But you wanted him to see them closer. It was a lovely sight on the solid ground above the towering cliffs. But there were better views to be seen.

Just south of the town was a little beach alcove, the waves were always calm there and the tide never seemed to come in. It perfectly faced the mainland— which really wasn't all that far from where you stood now. If it was anything like last year, you would be able to see the reflection of the lights on the water.

You carried through the square, moving away from the small buildings and toward a grassy cliff face— there was a set of uneven stone stairs that led down to the beach. Which you could see now at the first step.

Russia turned and glanced at the town behind. Though why, you weren't sure. Maybe he was confused at why you were still walking— and leading him down a set of stairs. You knew he could see the rolling hills of the land beyond from where he stood. He must have believed you were leading him there.

But you didn't think much of it. You simply kept stumbling down the slickened stone steps, warning him they were a little slippery as you went.

The beach below was shadowed completely. The grainy sand seemed black under the shade of the cliffs. It was cold and dry when you stepped out onto it. The sand beneath you crunching as you went.

You could hear Russia shuffling to catch up, muttering gibberish in his native tongue as he kicked in vain to get the sand off his shoes.

You stopped in the centre of the beach, smiling as you watched him. He grumbled as he stopped beside you, shuffling his feet as he shook loose specks off him.

You rolled your eyes and looked back at the mainland.

They finally turned the lights on.

The sea parted at the docks beyond. The vivid coral peaking from under the waves, revealed by the light that rippled on the water's surface. The dark churning of the sea met the yellow and white of the fairy lights swirling around poles and swaying in the air. The hills and homes further beyond silhouetted behind the humdrum of dull fluorescence. The small round bulbs shone like stars unable to reach the sky— suspended above a darkened world of night— bright and dull as they twinkled in your eyes.

It was just as wonderful as it was every year.

It was your favourite part of the season. You found yourself excited to see it every new Christmas that came around. This time, however, you weren't watching them alone.

You turned to the man beside you.

His white eyes were wide, lips agape. The twinkle of the lights pulsed in his sclera's, his breath caught in his own lungs.

For the first time since you met him, he looked genuinely happy.

W W   s

- -

C HAPTER 10

In the year your father died, you turned eighteen.

You wanted to do something with your life. Something great, something that would make you want to keep living on— something worth living for.

You kept an eye on the ad listings, you would walk through your small quaint town in your spare time, looking through shop windows for advertisements, searching for the words; 'We're hiring!' wherever you could find.

Until finally, on accident, you saw a job posting for a lighthouse keeper in the daily newspaper.

When you told your father about it, he was in the hospital. He had been battling dementia for a while by then. His condition was worsening. He hadn't recognised you in the previous visits, yet he constantly asked you, 'Where is (□/□)? Is (□/□) coming to visit me today?' His eyes wide and confused— not a single ounce of recognition in sight.

But when you showed him the paper with tears in your eyes, telling him you found a job and a place to live. He met your gaze, eyes steady, he had recognised you in that moment.

"That's the place you died, isn't it?"

He said.

And died.

Yet there you stood, alive and well, all these years later, watching Russia try and tell Maya that he was not writing love letters to Germany, and failing miserably.

You were doubled over the counter of Marla Connie's till, laughing uncontrollably as Russia argued with the little girl. His face red with embarrassment.

After a week and a few, the seamstress had finally finished tailoring new clothes for the Country, which you had come to pick up with him.

"He seems like he's settled in nicely, doesn't he?" Marla asked, chuckling away to herself as she rung up your money. "I think he has." You agreed, wiping tears from your eyes as you sighed audibly.

Marla leaned over the counter and little, her eyes watching her daughter clinging to the Russian's leg across her shop. "Say, he seems to be really good with Maya, if you wouldn't mind, maybe there could be some days I use him as a babysitter, if you don't have him working to the bone that is."

You thought it over. It could be good for him to have a job like that. As of now, you had finally managed to convince him to do small tasks around the lighthouse— which he took to just fine. Washing up, cleaning, lighting the Stanley when it got cold and doing laundry made up the bulk of his chores, and he got it all done before you finished your own work, leaving him with plenty of spare time in the day. Before, all his time was spent drinking and mulling around, now he spent his extra time playing card games with you and annotating the wildlife book he borrowed from you.

He spent his daylight hours prancing around outside, trying to find every flora and fauna in the meadows. Once found he would put a sticky note on the page in his book and circle it, proudly counting off everything he'd seen that day on a small notebook you lent him.

You thought it sweet that he had begun to collect wildflowers, drying them out in the kitchen and leaving them in bunches by his bed.

You liked that he spent his time now doing something other than drinking himself into a hole every evening.

It seemed as though he was getting a little better, finally having found the energy to do something more than sleep and think. But you were aware that this stage of recovery was fragile, so you made sure to give him as much of your time as you could, so he had less of it alone with his thoughts.

"I think that could be arranged, I'll bring it up with him." You agreed, smiling humbly to yourself, watching as the Russian was backed into a corner, desperately trying his hardest to tell the little girl he was still single, that he was not cheating on America with Germany.

You couldn't help but laugh some more as he looked in your direction, begging with his eyes for you to save him from more embarrassment.

You would have loved to watch this show all day, but you had other things to do, and Russia looked about five seconds from dropping to his knees and begging to whoever would listen to release him from the little girl's interrogation.

"Alright well, we better be off, thanks again for the clothes." You called to Marla over your shoulder, gesturing to Russia to follow as you did.

Russia let out an audible sigh of relief and inched away from Maya, jogging up to you. "It's no problem, I'll see you around (□/□)!" The seamstress exclaimed, waving as you grasped the door handle, listening to the sound of Maya complaining on your way out.

Russia let a loud desperate breath out his mouth, straightening his back, popping his spine in exasperation. "Zank God zat's over." You laughed and turned to him as you walked through the town square, swinging the bags of clothes all the while. "You're really good with kids."

Russia shrugged, cracking his knuckles as the two of you stopped. "I don't even know how." He mumbled, drawing another laugh from you.

You weren't all that sure what to do now. You had done all the things you had needed, now there wasn't anything left. Living in such a small quaint place meant there was little to do, so once all the things you knew you needed were over and done with, you had a tendency to just turn in for the night. But you really didn't want to promote that sad lifestyle to someone who only just seemed to be getting happier.

You swung the bags as you thought of what you could do with him.

That day he found three new flowers.

Cheddar pinks, bellflowers and dog roses.

One of each was hanging in your kitchen now, drying over the windowsill, preserving in the beat of the fiery Sun.

It would take a few days for them to dry out completely, to be preserved of their vivid colours, their scent of fresh petals.

"Afternoon (□/□), quite the day today, isn't it?"

You turned and waved back at Elizabeth Willow— the local florist walking past towards her home. A basket of fresh seeds looped in her arms, her smile wide. "Let's hope it stays this way." You called back, beaming from ear to ear.

The woman said nothing more, continuing her journey home, swaying her basket— just as you did your bags.

"How are you so komfortable talking to so many different people all time?" Russia asked from beside you, gazing down at you with his darkened lids. You shrugged. "Shouldn't you be used to it, given you're a country and all?"

But Russia just kicked his feet.

Maybe you should show him the garden Elizabeth took care of. If he kept up his botanical side hobby, he may like to see what a professional has to say about it. But that would be kept for another day, Elizabeth seemed busy, preparing for the bouquets she would have to put together for the winter celebrations.

Even then, you didn't wish to belittle him by showing him something similar to what he enjoyed, only done better by someone who knew what they were doing.

"So where are ve going now?" Russia suddenly perked up, choosing to look around as you did the same. Desperately trying to come up with something nice for the two of you.

You couldn't help but stare out at the sea.

The Sun, still high in the sky, wafting over the rumbling waves which swayed and rolled in your ears— a hint of salt in your nose and the gleam of light over the water in your eyes.

Seagulls cawed above your head, flying up towards the fire alight in the sky, the sea burning beneath you, clashing against the cliffs edge.

"We can get pastries and watch the passing ships if you'd like?" You offered, still staring at the shimmering water rocking back and forth.

Russia looked down at you.

The Sun in your eyes.

"I'd like zat."

D F T B

C HAPTER 11

Russia stared into the calm water below.

The blue ripples chugging past, parting against rocks, dragging leaves and sticks in its path. The gurgle of a small waterfall bellowed from elsewhere, the rush of water in his ears— the beat of the Sun on his skin.

He shuffled his weight onto the other leg. Hands meeting each other with loose fingers, a cigarette between two. Ash fell slowly, then became entrapped in the waters current, following it downstream.

He leaned his elbows further on the bridge, hunching his shoulders as he sighed, taking another pull.

From way below him, in the race of the water, he could see his own reflection— his white eyes staring up at him, as though it were someone else.

The day was resplendent, the Sun high, the birds chirping, the water warm.

But he was opposed.

Today was his first meeting in the UN since his father died. His first time having to speak for himself, in front of so many like him— yet so glaringly different.

He dressed up well for the occasion— a black and white wool suit he inherited from his father. He wanted to look presentable, so they thought much more of him. So he could sit back after it was all over and feel proud he was him— not anyone else.

For the past ten minutes, he had been stood there, going through cigarette after cigarette, practising what to say to the other Countries over and over again— until it was all he could hear in the back of his mind.

But all the good that did him was make him more nervous. He had gone in before, sure, but back then he was there with his father, a hand at the cuff of his pockets, his face hidden behind the older man's legs. Back then he didn't have to speak, but now, as he stood there, waiting for his anxiety to quell like it was a dying fire, he knew he would have to introduce himself.

All his brothers did— but that didn't make him feel less jittery.

He could feel his heart pounding in his head and his mind aching in his stomach. He could feel the grass under his dress shoes, the bridge under his elbows, the smoke in his eyes.

He could feel the breeze and the Sun on every inch of his skin— over the expense of his tailored suit.

He had to calm himself before he went in, he couldn't let anyone see him so worked up. What time was it anyway? It must be nearing the moment he would have to introduce himself to everyone— new and old, those who had met him as a child and those who were as new as he was.

Russia closed his eyes and drew a breath of his fag, the shadow of someone else falling to his left.

He opened his eyes again, and looked to see the person next to him.

"It's a lovely day, isn't it?"

You smiled at him, a pastry in your hands, your back against the bench the two of you sat on together. Russia parted his lips to answer, but was cut off by your excited voice exclaiming, "Red!" As another coloured boat sailed past.

Russia looked back out to sea, the waves bet against the body of the little rowboat— a crimson dot against the vast blue of depths beyond land. "It is." He answered, watching as the little rowboat went on— drifting like the clouds in the sky, off to some unknown land, its journey easy.

As an oddity to winter— it was a lovely day. The Sun couldn't stop smiling— hadn't stopped since he arrived. Clouds were thin and sparse, more like decoration in the blue sky than anything more. Jewels stitched into a garment of cobalt linen far above the reach of hands. The waves quiet and calm, lapping at the alcove— swinging by its lonesome at the horizon.

He watched it sway with you, counting the colours of boats that rowed past, over the lulling waves rocking themselves to sleep— a freshly baked pastry in both his and your hands, their aroma carrying in the breeze.

"What were you thinking about just now? You went really quiet for a while." You spoke suddenly, interrupting the crash of waves as the tide came in again. Russia shrugged. "Nothing, zis just reminded me of something."

"What was it?" You asked, tilting your head toward him, taking another bite, nodding your head all the while. "Nothing, really, it vas nothing."

Then the two of you turned back.

The little rowboat was further away now. A tiny red dot amongst the endless blue from above and below. A singular rose in an everglade of dripping stalactites— a singular dob of paint on a water-washed page.

Russia watched it pull back and forth, slow as it moved over the lapping water— attending to its diligent duty in far-off land. A world away from where he stood, a journey he watched, yet never met. A sonderous clarity flooded amongst his seated figure, his unmoving life witnessing the shift of time from other eyes.

He took another bite of his pastry.

"What was your life like?" You asked, quelling the silence stretching between the two of you, drawing his eyes onto yours. "My life?" He questioned, somewhat surprised at the suddenness of it. You nodded. "Yeah, back home."

He snuffed out his cigarette.

Staring deep into the eyes of United Nations.

The man smiled, shuffling to stand beside him, staring down from the bridge— just the same as Russia.

"Are you nervous?" He asked. Watching as the water flooded calmly by, the songbirds chirping their pretty tune from way up high in the canopies above. "Little." Russia confided, furrowing his brows as his fingers gripped the stone bridge— slick yet dry under the pelt of the flaming Sun.

UN smiled at him, his unblemished face soft and aglow in the nice weather. The blue covering of his skin contrasting all the greens around him nicely— like a red boat on a blue sea. "You shouldn't be, everyone is more than happy to work with you and your brothers. I can promise you there is nothing to worry about."

Russia's brows furrowed more— then relented. His face relaxing as he felt the need to smile. "Zank you. I kan't vait to vork vith everyone too."

UN smiled more, turning away to face the water— which held the same vibrance of his own skin.

"I'll make sure you have a good run," He assured.

"You can count on me."

Russia could never have imagined in that moment, when he smiled over the bridge. That UN would abandon him here. That all those nerves— the ones that kept him at the riverside, would never go away.

Russia blinked.

And took another bite.

"It vas good— vell as good as jumping betveen meetings and papervork is." He answered, shrugging all the while.

You nodded, like you were contemplating his reply, then moved on to the next question. "What was your childhood like?"

'Hey Rossiya! Get in vith us!'

Splashing and wading sounded through the chasm of songbirds and breeze. The laughter of kids as they stood one moment— then disappeared the next. Under the calm lid of crystal blue water. Grass blades dunking their tender leaves under as droplets came their way, splashed with the kids as they dove and resurfaced— laughing all the while.

'I'm okay zanks.'

The blanket he sat on crinkled as he shuffled. The aroma of chamomiles engulfing the fresh breeze, carried with the moss pores and fungus steaming from trunks of sycamores. Sparrows diving and twisting through the cobalt sky— meeting each other in unions of talons as they fell while the sky raised higher. Clouds chugging past like smoke— puffing up and thinning out, like petals unfurling.

The boy who called to him frowned, then went on playing. The water swallowing him— the tender cold quelling the incessant heat, protecting his skin from the many midges dancing on the surface. Hoards of dotted flies spinning in circles above him and the others— just as parched as they were.

Russia lowered his head back to his book— and continued reading.

Ambience of splashing careened in his ears, laughter from other mouths as he sat in silence. Red Admiral's danced by— their bright wings catching the Sun as they flew with the Sparrows.

The Sun opened wide. The breeze whispered to the grass.

He closed his eyes in the mellow of Summer.

"If you don't mind me asking." You reiterated, bringing him back for a moment.

His eyes opened.

He saw hands holding his body up— some sort of static blurring his vision, his legs limp on the ground behind him.

There was a dripping from somewhere in the room.

A cold reverberation splashing downward from a wooden panorama. An endless choke of ambience tumultuously spilling from somewhere— but he couldn't tell where.

Drip.

It blared as he shut his eyes, locking them tight— only listening to the indoor rain. The groan of the floorboards as he shuffled his weight left and right. His elbows buckling— screaming sounded from behind it all.

Drip.

Music lulled at his ears from somewhere else— sounding so near, yet so far all at once. Peace in other arms refusing to lift him into them. Abandoning him as his arms shook in agony— burning despair racking his head. The Sun gone and darkness the only false light that met the walls.

His eyes slowly opened again, the static in his eyes relenting.

Drip.

It was all over now.

He felt his elbows buckle again, almost dropping him into the pool of blood dripping from his lips. But he held his arms up, trying his hardest to push himself up and onto his knees.

But he just couldn't do it.

It was over now at least.

But if it truly was—

then why was the screaming getting louder?

"Niet." He found himself mumbling. Twisting his pastry around in his hands. His body leaning on his elbows, his back bent and uncomfortable. "It's okay."

He found his eyes gazing back out to sea.

The boat was gone now— the only one in the vast openness of untamed calling, vanished. Gone toward where it needed to be— away with the wind. "Vell, I don't know where to start," Russia mumbled, scrunching his shoulders up, before he dropped them low again. "It vas something. Zat's apparent."

He thought about what he could and couldn't say. What he wanted to, and what he just didn't.

You were staring at him now. He could feel your eyes in his peripheral. But he wouldn't turn to meet you, not without saying something first. So he dug through every little memory he had left— then met your gaze. "I am oldest of fourteen if zat ansvers your question."

Your eyes widened, your lips agape in a subtle smile that drowned out the anticipation Russia had been feeling. "Fourteen!? What is your mum? A spider?"

Russia laughed— the sound bounding through the loose breeze blowing between. His body straightening up again and leaning back, his face a little hot. "Niet, most of us had different Mamas."

Your head tilted— brows furrowed as you seemed to take an interest in his words. "Really?"

Russia nodded. "Yeah. I'm only fully related to Moldova, Ukraine, Belarus and Kazakstan. The rest had different Mamas zan us." He explained as he counted off on his fingers.

"Did you have a good relationship with them all?"

Eyes met his from the ground.

Deep and soulful— as they had always been. Inquisitive to a T and more observant than the Moon's shine. They searched and searched, over and over and over again, looking for something— but unable to find a glimpse of it.

'I don't ever vant to see you again.'

They then turned away. Those eyes elsewhere now, closed unto the darkening night— the twilight of passing time that left nothing in its wake. An endless march of passage splitting off at the present before him— leaving him in a past he couldn't escape, and a future he didn't wish to see.

Russia blinked.

"Yeah. Pretty good." He replied, taking another bite of his pastry, moving a palm to catch the little crumbs that dropped. "What about you? Do you have any siblings?" He asked as he turned to face you.

You nodded. "Yeah, I have an older sister."

"She is here?" Russia asked, shuffling his body so he could see you better through the light that shone down in ribbons.

"No, she's on the mainland." You mumbled, turning away towards the sea again.

There were no more boats out there. Having already sailed far away, towards a land away from there, ignoring the lives watching from afar. It was just blue now— deep, patient blue stretching up and down, everywhere but where he stood. Its light unreached.

"Does she ever kome to visit you?" He asked, still staring towards you, expecting the same from you. But you clutched your pastry closer to yourself, and half-heartedly laughed, shaking your head. As if you found his words funny in some way. "Sometimes I see her, not often though."

Russia turned away again. "Zat's shame."

Then there was the sound of silence— carried by the breeze. Interlocking fingers with the branches and blades, holding hands with the horizon and dancing across the surface of the water. Twinkling in the high Sun, the royal quietude that found its place in everything, ruling over the birds as they quelled their singing— the waves seemed so far away.

You were the first to break it. Though you never looked towards him— and he never looked towards you. "Is there anything I can do to make you feel completely at home here?"

Russia's head shook automatically, his body leaning forward again to rest his elbows on his knees. "You shouldn't have to do zat."

You cut in rather quickly, as if knowing he would end up going on a rant about how you were already doing too much. How he appreciated everything you did, but ultimately, didn't deserve any of it. "I'd like to do it. I want you to feel like you belong here, y'know?"

Russia gripped his pastry harder, his head down toward the ground— he couldn't help but speak before he really thought. "Just being vith you feels homely enough." He mumbled.

He saw you smile in his peripheral. One hand on the wooden bench— the other raising to take a bite of your pastry.

There was no reason why he did it.

Perhaps, a silent note in his mind wanted to thank you, but he hadn't the words to express it. He hardly noticed he did it at all— until he felt it on his own skin. The slight tingle as he set his hand above yours, a friendly gesture of camaraderie, a thank you in his own strange way.

He was praying you wouldn't mention it. And in the end, it didn't matter. You had as little to say as he did, as it so seemed. You merely kept your eyes off his, towards the blue sea beyond.

There were no boats anymore. But that didn't matter.

The only sonder he cared about now, was the shared understanding between him, and the one next to him.

Nothing else mattered.

D R ;IL Y

C HAPTER 12

□□□□□□□□□□ □□□□□□□□□□— □□□□□□□ □□□ □□□□□□: 1,819.

'□□□□ □□□□.'

'£□□ □□□□.'

'□□□□□ □□□□□□□.'

'□□□□□ □□□□□ □□□□.'

You wound the mechanic rotation. The lantern room lit up in bright rays of yellow and auburn. The light spun and flashed— as though it was repeating Morse code to whatever ships may pass in the night.

Its unique words written in fiery calligraphy— unique to its own, unlike any other lighthouse in the world.

You turned on the battery-powered transmitter— keeping its sound on max, the speaker on, in the unlikely situation, that a ship would find trouble, and requested help in the night.

You backed away from the mechanisms and cold metal of the lantern— the sudden flashing lights scorching your eyes, and looked out to sea.

It was dark now, but the water was still as calm as the day, the slight wind that picked up brushed against the surface— leaving the expanse of waves undisturbed as it went.

From the long, windowed walls hugging the entirety of the lantern room, you could just about make out another ship. A rather large vessel that reminded you of a ferry— armoured and hefty as its barge broke the waves parting under it.

You watched its grey and white body slowly chugging through the water. Bobbing and swaying as it powered on through the night.

When you saw ships this late, you always liked to imagine they were grateful for you. That the little work you did in the lonesome of the encased archipelago you lived on, was worth something in a larger sense. Your work was bigger than you— at least you liked to tell yourself. It made you proud to be who you were in that moment. To stand and watch them go by, knowing you were now a part of their little journey— something greater than your life as it was.

You turned away, and descended down the spiral staircase, sighing exhaustedly as you went. Woefully prepared to drop into your bed, and let the day be forgotten to the next.

You swung yourself around on the railing, stopping in the middle of your shared room, your bed in front of you, but your body facing the centre.

Russia had come back with you after both had finished the pastries. Though he said he wasn't tired, and as you ascended to the lantern room to do your due diligence, he wandered off into the evening, saying he wanted to find someplace new.

Usually, during the day, he crossed the island to get to Dartmouth Meadow— which lay just behind the town. It was quite the walk, so he found it was better during the day, as that would leave him with more time to explore. But after you showed him a map of your little island, he realised he could always take a quicker walk to the Cherry-bark woods— just north of your lighthouse.

You hadn't told him it was too late to go outside, that during the night the wind usually picked up and there was always the terrifying chance a gust would blow him towards the edge, and off the cliffs below.

But he had seemed so excited to see what it was like there, so you chose not to scare him off— if he would even listen anyway.

With the map you leant him in hand, he excitedly explained all the places he was going to go over the time he was here.

Maybe sometime, on a nice day, he would take a dip in Cornflower Lake— or ascend to the highest peaks of the Mallow Mountain Range, or maybe how he would cross Dartmouth Meadow and build sand forts on the east side beach.

It never failed to bring a smile to your face when he so happily talked about all the little places on your island, running through plans he made without much thought— inviting you on his little escapades.

You had to turn this one down. Saying you would show him the rest another time. Your duties couldn't wait, and your rest— even less so.

As you stood facing the middle of the room, you realised how tussled and unmade his bed was. You huffed at his neglect and walked forth, pulling his duvet back to flap out the crinkles and lay it neatly back.

The floral linen met your eye, the pretty unblemished hand-me-downs your grandmother gave you years ago. They were just as you remembered as a child.

Only— your heart sank when you saw them.

It wasn't nostalgia that bled through your chest— the remnants of a time passed you recognised through a much older lens. It wasn't the calm memory of the fleetingness of time and the creeping of age.

It was the little imperfections stained into the covers.

Drops of blood pooled around stitched flowers. Red stains tracing petals— the natural world meeting the inner workings of a man as he lay still— unknowingly falling into the mattress, melting into the cotton as he slept.

Your heart sank further.

The dread of realisation eating you alive.

A companion's worst nightmare as you realised maybe, you had been wrong. Maybe, he wasn't getting better, he was only hiding it more thoroughly.

You pulled the duvet back completely.

It was only around the top of his mattress, where his arms would rest in the night. You understood then why he wore bandages under his jumpers. Why he never pulled his sleeves up. Why he always turned in the night, as though no position he laid in was comfortable.

You backed away from his bed, your heart in your ears— your mouth dry and throat clenching.

You turned frantically, trying to find somewhere else that had the same stains, perhaps it was just a one-time thing? Maybe he got cut up by thorns in the meadow one day, maybe it was nothing at all.

You bent down to pick up one of his jumpers at the end of his bed, turning the sleeve inside out to pry further.

You hated what you found.

Stains that had been there so long they were brown at the edges, crusted and hanging onto loose linen. You dropped it and probed further.

Smears were subtly visible on his half-drunk vodka bottle— pressed in by fingertips as he held it close to his body, though now left on his nightstand to dry in the room's breeze.

You put it back with uneven hands. Your stomach feeling sick.

Had he been lying? You were so woefully convinced he was getting better. That every day he spent out and in the Sunshine were doing him good. That you were taking care of him— like you promised you would. Were you not doing a good enough job? Was what you were offering him, somehow making him feel worse?

Was it your fault he was miserable?

You backed up, then took off down the stairs. Throwing the door of your lighthouse open you stood in the darkened world, the ground eerily lit by the lantern miles above you.

You stomped through the grass, around your home and to the outhouse.

There was nothing in the world you were more sensitive to than things like these. There was a certain harm that came along with it— to everyone involved. When someone believes so strongly their soul is dirty and heavy, that they conceive of an escape plan so painful.

You hated to think he would do the same thing your sister did.

All that joy that comes with love and admiration— snuffed out simply because you failed to ask what they were thinking, how they really felt.

You reached the outhouse, with the plan to retrieve bleach and a spare sheet for him. To wash away anything that might remind him of his actions. To make it a little easier to forget about the strain of misery.

You knew better than to leave him by himself in all this.

You miss one call then—

Poof.

You opened the door. And it reminded you so clearly of what happened before. This was your nostalgia— hanging in front of your eyes as you stared into the outhouse. Your treasured loved one, on display like a wax figure. So recognisable in that moment, yet so uncanny now there was no light behind her eyes. Now that her feet were off the ground. Now that she was blue— inside and out.

It's all over.

And there was so much you could do to stop it.

But you just couldn't find the time.

You blinked. And walked through the doorway.

Next to the toilet in front of you was a mesh basket full of cleaning supplies. You stalked towards it and dug through, pulling a bottle of bleach from the fragrances and polish. Then stood right back up.

But that wasn't enough, was it?

Merely cleaning up what he had done just wasn't good enough. How would that make him feel? He hadn't done anything wrong, not really. In his mind, he was doing what he had to do. Something that drew him from his agony and gave him a reason to be the way he was— to feel the way he felt.

It wasn't fair to make him feel as though he was doing something wrong. That what he was doing was somehow disgusting— wasteful.

You sighed, staring at the bottle, trying to come up with something to do for him. Something nice— something that he would appreciate.

You had the foresight to prevent it this time. And you would be a fool to deny it.

When you first moved into the lighthouse, you had a habit of forgetting where to put things, so you made the smart decision of buying sticky notes and placing them around your home— writing little reminders for yourself. Maybe, he would appreciate that the same as you had.

You dragged your heels up to the mirror on your right, then opened the medicine cabinet above. Inside were the obvious things, but tucked away in the corner was a little sticky notepad, still with a handy pen next to it.

Then began writing things on them.

You weren't sure what to write, you hadn't a clue what he needed to hear— nor what it was he wanted. But you had a feeling it was simple.

All he needed to hear, was that you appreciated him. That you needed him in your life, that everything was going to be alright in the end— you would make sure of it.

The concept was simple. In shaky, brief cursive, you wrote the only thing that came to mind. All the little notes beginning with the same phrase.

□□□□□ □□□□□□□□.

Then you finished it off with a sweet semblance. Something you wished to say before time caught up— and you would never get the chance to.

Simple words— that meant more than all the riches in the world.

□ £□□□ □□□.

□'□ □□□□□ □□ □□□.

□ □□□□□□□□□□ □□□□□□□□□□ □□□'□□ □□□□□.

You placed the pen down. Staring at the little notes— your handwriting was crooked and leaning to one side, but it didn't matter. You made a promise to take care of him, and thats exactly what you were going to do.

With cramped fingers, you stuck one to the mirror. Hoping he'd see it the next time he was in there.

Then you gathered up the notes, the bleach, and grabbed a spare bedsheet from the cupboard— and left the outhouse.

Once you got back inside, you stopped in the kitchen to place one on the railing— opposite where he usually sat when he came in. Hoping he'd see it when he was at his lowest.

You continued upstairs, and placed another on his bedside lamp— the old gas-powered light he never seemed to use. And just to be safe, in case he missed that one, you put one on his bottle of alcohol— right next to his gas lamp.

You stood back and examined what you had done.

Was this too much? Or too little? You weren't sure if he would even appreciate it, he didn't seem the type. But it eased your mind, and until you found out how he felt about it— it took a little of that weight off your chest.

In a bundle of cloth, you dropped the linen on the floor, tossing the bottle of bleach on top. Now you had to strip his bed, and change it for him.

But you didn't mind.

All that mattered— in every minute that flew past, from your eyes, was that when he got back, he wouldn't plummet into some kind of vat.

You didn't know how to swim— but you could help him float.

May God despise your efforts— but find you in the currents.

$$C \qquad\qquad O$$

- -

C HAPTER 13

300 years ago.

A singular seed found an area of dented ground. A soft spot in the Earth— watered and cared for by the clouds above.

Nestled comfortably in its bed of humus and leaves— it sprouted. Growing larger and larger as time passed to decades— entire centuries told by the rings it grew inside.

It saw what we call history, and what itself saw as passing time. Countless Sunsets reached forth and bathed its leaves, hundreds of nights it saw through in the bitter cold and rain.

Even once humanity sunk their claws into the land its roots held together, it stood forever unmoving— forevermore it would stand.

Walking through them all, each and every trunk older than planes and cars and civilisation as it is now. Unfathomable in ordinary minds, but so ordinary to its own.

Something that could stand for this long, still blooming in the spring, still sleeping in the winter— something such as this. Did we even really deserve it? To see a monument we overlook too easily, a test of time slipped through our fingers, nothing more than a witness that had no mouth, a curator that had no eyes.

Time didn't change them. They were still the same as they were, centuries ago— only older now.

Darker, approaching the end of time in their eyes. Their last Sunsets upon them, the burn of a horizon beckoning, calling to them, inviting them to fall, to create something new from the same old routine they always revisited.

Wouldn't that be nice?

For a duty to come to an end, after slaving under the Sun for so long.

At least in the twilight, they would be given some peace of mind. A chance to rest, for now, then continue.

Russia weaved in between them— thinking all the time. Traipsing through the museum of wood surrounding him. Looking for something, anything he hadn't seen before. A ruby in the dirt, amongst the colosseum rising towards the Heavens.

There was a breeze in the air, a little wisp of a wind, but it wasn't at all heavy. It blew through the twigs and branches, rustling in the wind as if playing a kind of off-key melody. A lullaby in the Moonlight— the only semblance of a torch he had with him, coupled with the afterglow of your lighthouse, way back at the cliffs.

He hadn't wanted to go home with you. He had too much on his mind— that little questionnaire you gave him got his mind thinking, and he had a feeling he wouldn't have enjoyed sitting in bed after, thinking of all the things he chose to say, and what he chose not to.

He thought this might quell his internal monologue, and hand him some peace of mind.

In a way it did.

Surrounded by a life form that had no way to acknowledge him— a being that couldn't judge, nor ask why he was still awake at a time such as this.

He liked that about the great outdoors. It was the only place where no one could really see him. He liked this island, it was steadily growing on him. But he was still struggling to get used to the fact that everyone knew more about him than he did them.

He hated their prying eyes and knowing smiles.

He hated that they knew what he had done, and the work he left behind.

But alone in the woods, engulfed by the Moon's light— surrounded by blades of grass, moss pathways and branches older than he could comprehend, he felt a little better about himself.

The entrails of beauty met his hands at every turn. The quiet rustling and squealing from somewhere else mollified his mind and calmed whatever nerves he had building up.

A small clump of colour caught his eye, shining under the Stars like a firefly.

He stalked towards it and dropped to his knees. Gently reaching out and touching its supple petals.

It was a dark pink— almost purple in colour. Shaped like the edges of Stars at the ends and dotted with green freckles all across its petals. Fingertips of buttercup reached out from its mouth at the centre and invited whatever may into its aromatic embrace.

Russia smiled a little, but only a little.

You would love this, wouldn't you?

You seemed to take an interest in his new hobby of dry flowers. You got a real kick from quizzing him on which flower was named what. He never got it wrong, but you held out for the idea that maybe one day, he would, and you would claim victory over the game you played seemingly with yourself.

As gently as he could, he ran his fingers down the pale green stem, and pressed his nail in, cutting it neatly, bringing it towards himself.

He stood back up, twirling it around in his fingers. He hadn't seen this one before, he didn't know its name. Maybe if you asked when he got back, you would finally catch him out, and win.

Russia couldn't stop his smile from growing.

It was still so quiet in the canopy. The night spilling its dark paint over the empty sky, Stars falling in clumps as they expanded outwards. Russia breathed a breath of fresh cold air.

It was nice out here.

Alone— no one to bother hi—

"What are you doing out here?"

Russia jumped and turned, stumbling over his own feet but catching himself on a trunk behind him.

"I kould ask you same." He spat, a little annoyed the person had ruined his perfect peace. But the person merely laughed, stepping a little closer so they could see him better. "I like midnight strolls, makes it easier to keep the town free of rubbish during the day." The person explained as they came into view.

Russia wasn't sure if he recognised her. She looked a lot older than you, perhaps early 30's. Her hair was tied back in a low ponytail, her arms crossed over her red jacket— zipped up tight to protect from the biting cold. He couldn't see her well enough to define much of her complexion, but he could just about make out her subtle smile in the Moonlight.

"I don't believe we've actually properly talked, have we?" She asked as she leaned back against a tree— her arms crossed all the while. "I don't zink so?" Russia responded, twirling the flower in his fingers nervously, feeling rather unnerved by the suddenness of her appearance.

"That's okay, my name is Sarah Kacey, I'm the mayor of this town." She explained, smiling as she spoke— her white teeth glistening through the darkness, a youthful sparkle in her eyes, despite her growing age.

"It's nice to meet you Ms." He mumbled back, but she merely chuckled and waved her hand, denying his formality. "Please just call me Sarah, I want you to see me as an equal, not a superior."

Russia nodded, turning away, trying to look anywhere but her. Wishing to still be left to his lonesome, to continue gathering his thoughts in the dead of night— in the peace he was only just discovering.

"What do you have there?" She asked, pushing herself off from the tree, coming closer to get a look at the flower he held in his fingers.

"Oh um, I'm not sure." He instantly felt stupid. She wasn't looking for a name, she must have been looking for a description. All he had to say was 'a flower' but no, there he went again with his stupidity. His nervous ticks of obvious answers and dismissal— the idiocy of his design.

But she didn't mind. She laughed again, holding her hand out to ask for it, and he gave it away without a second thought.

She twirled it in the Moonlight, holding it up to get a better look, before she set it back into his hands— still with that same smile on her lips. "Looks like a hellebore to me." She explained as he took it from her outstretched fingers. Examining it with his own eyes.

"Did you get it for (□/□)? She would like that."

Russia felt his face heat up, his hands retreating to his body, as if to hold himself in some way. "Niet, I just like vay zey look." He bumbled, tumbling over his own words as he spoke— drawing another light laugh from her.

"Are you settling in alright?" She asked, changing the conversation topic— saving him the embarrassment.

Russia turned away, somehow feeling more awkward than before. "Yeah, I zink I am."

Sarah's smile waned a little, as if for a moment, she remembered something. A conscience in the back of her mind that shone through in a small sliver of a moment. "You ought to be good to that girl, she's had a rough life." She mumbled, staring him down with her deep brown eyes, telling him even without words she was being serious.

His fingers rolled the flower in his hands. His mind registering what it was she said. Then his throat replied. "What do you mean by zat?"

Sarah shook her head, her arms crossed again, her eyes on the ground momentarily. "It's not my place to tell." She muttered, stepping back by an inch. "She was just desperate and ended up here, that's all you should know."

Russia didn't react, nor did he think about it too much. Like Sarah said—it wasn't his place to know. If you wanted to tell him, you would. Prying did nothing for anyone, only drawing distrust between the two parties involved.

He would hate to find you snooping about his business— it worked both ways.

"But anyway, you should get back to her, she always thought that lighthouse was a lonely place, she must need the company and it seems you need it too," Sarah announced out of the blue, her smile now gone, but her spirit never faltering.

Russia self-consciously twirled the Hellebore in his fingertips again, then stepped back, Sarah did the same, beginning to turn away. "Zanks for the chat," Russia called as he walked away, Sarah turned and waved her hand high— her smile back. "Anytime! If you have any questions or concerns, it's my job to listen!" She declared as she turned fully, continuing her quiet midnight walk through the woods.

Russia turned away, and began back towards the lighthouse— guided by the flashing fluorescence that lit up the surrounding area way up in the canopy.

The night was older now. A cold breeze sent a shiver down his spine— the only ambience for miles being his footsteps along the muddy terrain. The occasional slip of a protruding root and rustle of the leaves swaying in the growing wind.

He followed the path of light through the dark, his hands meeting trunks to ensure he wouldn't trip. The pretty flower locked tight but loose in his fingers, its presence bringing him some company as he walked alone.

Then, the lighthouse came into view. Its towering body soaring above the canopy, the lantern spinning and flashing as it went. Inviting him towards the safety of its walls.

He walked around it, and opened the door.

It was silent inside, though a cosy sort of warm. He listened to the clank of his footsteps as he made his way upstairs, intending to call to you, to announce that he was home. But he didn't do that— for worry that you were already asleep. He didn't wish to disturb you if you were. But just to be safe, he walked all the way up to the bedroom to check on you.

He was right, you were dead asleep. Your hair being the only thing sticking up from your duvet.

He smiled a little, then went back down a flight to the kitchen, where he planned to hang the Hellebore up to dry alongside the rest of the vibrant flowers.

A chill came in through the closed window above the table. A small sliver of filtered light shining as the Moon gazed into the cramped space. He saw the rest of his collection outlined against it— hung upside down by their stalks, crisping in the Moonlight.

He tied a little of the loose ribbon around the Hellebore, then left it to hang alongside the rest of them— standing back to admire its pretty petals.

His eyelids grew heavy as he gazed, and he felt the desire to crawl into bed, joining you in a world that never met.

He yawned as he turned, putting a hand to his mouth.

Then stopped.

He noticed it immediately, stuck to the railing in front of his eyes— a vibrant square laced with black ink in the most beautiful calligraphy. It drew him towards it, he couldn't help himself as he picked it up— and read it.

And that was how his heart broke.

Standing there— alone. An intruder into a life that wasn't made for his inclusion. A collector of beauty that strung them up and found passion in their death. A spring-locked trap awaiting some sort of natural admiral to come across him— and perish in what he was.

A vat of despair.

Someone who could so easily convince himself he was happy. Just because he was scared someone would care that he wasn't.

Drips of tears hit the paper in his fingers. He couldn't stop himself from raising it, and burying his closed eyes against it. Shoulders shaking all the while— body curling forwards like it was caving in.

Despair racked him from the inside, and instead of denying it like he had been teaching himself to do— he let it take over him.

Cold hands with hot fingers ran molten through his frozen veins. Falling down into the crevice of his soul and up into the folds of his mind. Burning despair aching in his chest— he did nothing to stop any of it.

He didn't deserve someone like you. Did he?

After everything he had ever done— to himself and those around him, he didn't deserve redemption.

He was the point of no return. The rockiness under some kind of rock bottom— the pit six feet under acceptance, the endless hole of depression he was woefully unable to claw out from.

The denial of joy that he was.

He didn't deserve anything you had done for him. He didn't deserve to be happy. Maybe if he stopped pretending he was, you would understand that there was no saving him.

He would never get better, would he?

T H   A T C

C HAPTER 14

There were a lot of things you loved about your home.

The spiral staircase, the warmth, the dim lighting, the position of it. But there was one thing you loved above all the others.

It wasn't because it was better than any of them. It was simply because you chose it yourself.

The mint painting of the walls.

When you moved in all those years ago, it was all white. If you had left it like that any longer, you would have gone insane. It wasn't far from padded walls of an asylum. If anything, it was interlinked.

The blandness of what it used to be like sent you spiralling every time you awoke. The monotony of your work seemed much more cruel when it was all one colour. Dim and sad— crumbling in the corners and flaking from the sides. Drywall collapsing onto your table— cracks over the skirting board.

It took a few months for you to finish painting.

But you would never regret it.

Now you awoke to a pretty room— decked out in all the little trinkets you collected over the years, stacked in front of the colour you chose, and applied yourself.

As you opened your eyes and blinked sluggishly, you could smell a sweet aroma wafting from downstairs. A light clatter as someone moved items around.

You turned your head to face Russia's bed, he wasn't there, but his bed had been neatly made, indicating he was the one downstairs.

You rubbed your eyes as you sat up, cracking your shoulders while you pulled on your arms and stretched your back out. Letting out a tired yawn.

You got up slowly, taking all the time you had to wake yourself up as you dressed and brushed out your hair. Constantly rubbing sleep from your tear ducts, your eyes adjusting to the morning Sun gleaming through the window.

You descended the stairs with uneven steps, leaning heavily on the railing as you went.

Russia was standing by the sink, hunched over something on the island in front of him. A sweet aroma filled the room— like sugar and nectar kneaded together in a palmed dough. He stood with his sleeves rolled up and his hat placed neatly on the counter beside him.

"Morning." You say as you enter the kitchen, waltzing up to the table and pulling a chair for yourself— sitting haphazardly in your dreary state. Russia turned with a phlegmatic smile. He looked utterly exhausted, and though you didn't want to say it aloud, it was the only thing you found you could concentrate on.

"Perfekt timing." He chirped, turning back to grab a plate of something, before he brought it over to you.

You couldn't help but let out an unexpected gasp. Your eyes wide— mouth-watering as you stared at the plate of freshly cooked pancakes, whipped cream dolloped on the side with maple syrup drizzled over blackberries sprinkled on top.

"What's all this for?" You gushed excitedly, lifting your knife and fork as he brought you a cup of tea along with it all. Before sitting down in front of you— lighting up one of the cigarettes you allowed him to take.

"A zank you." He said— smiling into his palm as he turned away— realising you had noticed the part he took the most time on.

It was a hard thing for him to do. He could hardly see when he wrote it out through the tears and sleep deprivation. The world around him seemed fallacious as he stood in the early morning light, placing his pride in the dark, so he may repay some kind of debt he felt he owed to you.

He didn't sleep last night. He couldn't have— usually, he was kept up in the twilight anyway, but always found his resting hours during the day. Hiding in his covers like a scared mouse unable to leave its burrow. But he wasn't able to do that here— the last thing he wanted was for you to worry more about him. You had enough burdens as it seemed.

"Well then, what's this one's name?" You asked slyly, smiling through your eyes. Russia didn't have to turn his head to know what you meant, he only hid himself further. "Hellebore."

You smiled wider— humbly as pushed your lips out, wishing to hide it.

Beside the lovely breakfast he made for you was a flower, dark pink in colour, a brown tag wrapped around its stem, the words, '□□□□□ □□□□□

□□□; □ □□□□□□□□□□ □□□□□□□□□□ □□□ □□ □□□ □□' was written in well-practised cursive.

You began eating in silence. The only ambience being the subtle sound of Russia as he breathed in the burning of his cigarette. It didn't escape you how he had made no breakfast for himself— but chose instead to have a fag. He may have made himself something earlier, but by the way his expression seemed so despondent, you weren't sure if he had.

"You didn't have to do this." You mumbled through bites of your pancake. He never looked in your direction, only lowering his head as he heard you speak in a hushed voice. "I vanted to." Was all he said— his eyes watching birds go by the window— soaring through the clouds like spinning tops. Dancing and weaving between each other— as free as the wind itself.

You said nothing more. Only eating quietly— smoke completing the room, sweet sugary aromas wafting through the burning stench— the complete union of two halves, either end of a spectrum meeting in the middle of the table. An ashtray for him, a plate of sweets for you. A cigarette and a flower, divided between its owners, a divorce of choices and actions.

You two seemed so different on the outside. You seated with the Hellebore at your side, a sweet treat at your fingertips— while he sat opposite, a cigarette between his fingers, an ashtray at his side.

But there was an understanding between the two of you. He was aware there was an anguished reason for your move here, while you knew the same of him.

The both of you were different— yet the same in some regard. A dissident to the past, standing between Heaven and Hell, where the ground met infernos and the sky met clouds. A land devoid of substance yet being the only home either of you could carve.

The only difference between the two of you—

He was unable to let go of the past, and allowed it to destroy him. Whilst you denied your past, and moved painfully along, lest you lose your mind.

You found ways to be happy, even if a part of it felt forced, but he couldn't even begin to look, there was nothing for him to find anymore.

You were the Hellebore, whilst he was the cigarette.

Eventually, you were to wilt when time was due, but he would always burn out, no matter what he did.

"Zank you."

"For notes."

You finished your breakfast and pushed the plate away. Russia put out his cigarette, leaving its burned remnants in the ashtray.

"It's no problem, you seemed like you needed them."

Russia kept his eyes on the table, his arms crossed against it. His hat was still off, left on the counter behind you. His hair was matted and unkept— you could see the exhaustion in his eyes. The swelling darkness in the glassy overcoat— the fatigue he felt within, burning out the glimmer that would have been. Dark-lined bags underneath, sinking his face inward.

"I want to help you Russia, but I can't do that if I don't know what's going on."

His eyes shut tight, his head falling more.

The sound of birdsong came in through the window. Gulls from the sea and pigeons from the woods— singing in the sky as they landed and jumped, taking flight towards the Sun, leaving the two of you behind for some greater land. A place everyone wished they could go, but would never meet with eyes so shallow.

"I don't know what's wrong."

You watched him shake his head, burying it in his hands, hiding what he saw as shame from you. There were no feelings within you but pity, you knew that's not what he wanted you to feel, but it was all you could. It was the only thing you could offer him— the empathy of understanding.

"I know about it, you don't have to be ashamed, it's okay."

But he regressed further, lowering his head to grip his hair in his fingers, his head shaking fervently, his hands shaking. Your pity began to build up, you wanted to reach out and take his hands in yours, to stand and pull him into you— telling him all the while that everything was okay, you were right here, there was still time for him to feel happy.

He seemed to believe this was the end of the world— this was the part of the book where the sky fell into the ground, the Moon expanding and drifting closer, the part where you turned the radio up on your favourite song and held his hand, watching as the sky cracked and shattered, everyone but you and him running for their lives— the moment of acceptance that this was his last day on Earth. And there was nothing he could do to escape it.

"...no."

He was out of time to feel happy.

Oxygen was waning— there was no longer anything for him to breathe, he would soon succumb as the sky tumbled down. No ground would swallow his body, no memorial or eulogy for him to be remembered. There was nothing at the end of the Earth. Everything was gone— no one would care if he went too.

That was all in his mind. But written all over his crestfallen figure.

"Please, I want to help you, please just show me what you've done so I can help you."

He began to cry into his hands. His shoulders shaking as his body lurched, throat gasping for breath he couldn't find— sobbing filled the room. The songbirds stopped completely, flying away from him, leaving an empty silence between each heartfelt gasp.

But you didn't know how to comfort him, you didn't know how to reach out and embrace him— you didn't know how to say with words that you cared in this moment. You only stared, your throat locking up, drowning the sobs that were minutes away from choking you. You wanted to hold him and tell him this wasn't the end of the world. And even if it was— you would be right beside him as the sea burned. A wreck of inflamed water sinking towards the depths, the horizon vanishing within the sky, your hand in his as you said goodbye to what was left.

But you didn't say anything.

There was nothing you could say.

There was nothing that could change his mind.

"I don't know why I do it. I don't understand what's wrong vith me."

He gripped his hair tight, tears hitting the table beneath him. His body pushing forward— almost collapsing, you leaned toward him, eyes struggling to latch onto one single thing.

"And that's okay. Sometimes there doesn't need to be a reason for anything. But it won't stay like that, nothing lasts forever— and that's okay too. You won't be unhappy for the rest of your life, you won't be happy for the rest of your life, that's the human experience. But I want you to know that you're not by yourself, I'm right here when you need me. I'd do anything for you if it meant you could be happy, even for just a moment."

He calmed his breathing, his fingers going limp. Slowly, he dropped his hands down, meeting your eyes with those unresponsive scleras, now red and puffy— glossy with tears, the only shine they would ever have, it seemed.

"Kould you hold me?"

You stood up without another word, and walked around the table, not wasting a moment in wrapping your arms around his head and pulling him in. He was tall enough so that even when you stood, he could just about reach up and set his head on your shoulder. His eyes watering all over again, his fingers fraught against your waist, pulling you desperately into him.

"You're the best zing zat ever happened to me."

You could hear a pigeon call outside the window. Deep and mellow, dragging its melancholic song through the breeze, entering the room like a gramophone playing elsewhere. You rested your head atop his.

"And I will always be here for you when you need me."

R   T   S

C HAPTER 15

"Just 3 for the lot please."

You pulled some cash from your pocket, handing it over to Rosalind Dona— the local baker, in exchange for a loaf of fresh bread.

As soon as you and Russia had stepped into the town square, Maya and Aiden had seen him, and made a beeline towards him, following under his feet as you walked into the bakery together.

They were with him now, across the shop, hounding him with all kinds of childish questions. Though you couldn't stop yourself from smiling as you realised they stopped asking if he was married to America— in place of asking if he was eloped to you now.

Rosalind packaged your bread whilst watching them with you, struggling in vain to hold in her laughter as Russia fought for his life against the two children.

The baker was an older woman— never once turning down the prospect of having a glass of red wine over gossip. Her brown hair tied in a new hairstyle every day, usually done up to mirror the loaves she was offering in her shop amongst the pastries and culinary ingredients.

Usually, her sister, Beatrice, helped run the place, but today it seemed, she was off somewhere with Peggy Jade— the barmaid at the local pub. You always liked Beatrice, and every time she was in, you had a lengthy conversation with her. Usually, it descended into Bea talking nonstop about her friend, as you were the only one on the island who knew she had a thing for her. Not even her own sister knew, but she trusted you enough to keep her secret.

"I think Russia really likes you," Rosalind stated as she pushed your bread across the counter, smiling at you, "If you're given the chance, I think you should leave with him."

You snorted, glancing towards the Russian to assure yourself he hadn't heard. But he seemed too preoccupied with getting his hat back off Maya without harming the little girl to notice anything else. "That's a weird way to say 'Here's your bread my dearly beloved customer.'"

Rosalind rolled her eyes, "Har har," she joked, leaning over the counter to stare down at Maya, before she was suddenly lifted by Russia— laughing and kicking her legs as he held her out like she was some kind of rabid animal. "But in all seriousness, you should think about it, he could be good for you, I mean, look how good he is with Maya, the child loves him."

You turned to look at Russia. He was busy threatening to throw Maya off the cliffs and into the waves, while she giggled like it was the best joke she ever heard.

"Yeah, he seems soooo good with her." You rolled your eyes and smirked at Rosalind, who was staring at you in her peripheral. "Okay ignore what he's saying and he's good with her." She reiterated, before laughing again.

"I'll think about it if it gets you off my case." You mumbled, sparing small glances back at Russia as you lifted the bread into your arms. "Could you do me a favour and tell Maya and Aiden to help you or something? We need to go to a few other places and I don't think Russia would want them under his feet the whole time."

Rosalind nodded and smiled, whistling loudly at the two kids to get their attention.

You tried not to laugh at them as they lined up like soldiers in front of the till, allowing Russia to sprint for the door and throw himself out before they followed.

You left behind him, listening to the sound of the baker giving orders to the kids— monotonous cleaning work that made them groan and complain.

"I hate children." Russia gasped as you joined him outside. He was constantly fixing his hat atop his head, trying to settle it comfortably after it was disturbed. "Those two are a lot I know." You laughed as you continued walking, Russia following right after.

"Where to now?" He asked, staring up into the great blue sky, the birds a plenty, not a trace of a cloud in sight. "The Post Office, I'd like to pick up a copy of the papers."

Russia hummed as you backtracked across the town square, past the pub and towards the post office.

Atop the face of the building, there was an old clock— a relic from the first settlers back in the late 1800's. It was the only way to tell the time on the island, unless you had some sense of utilising the Sun. But you found it impossible to tell eleven in the morning from noon. You could tell morning from afternoon, and evening from night— the rest was told by the old Post Office clock.

As it stood now, it was 1:43– the Sun was high, the day still young. There was plenty of time for you and Russia to make plans on doing something fun together.

You were thinking of bringing him up to Cornflower Lake in the later day. He had expressed interest in it before, and with the warm Sun and cloudless sky, today seemed perfect for a cooling down in the water.

But for now, you were doing the rounds for needed items.

You stepped up to the old brick walls of the Post Office, pushing open the wooden door that creaked and spluttered. The building was one of the oldest on the island, having survived after all the others were damaged during the second war— when your island had been mistakenly bombed. As Sarah had passionately told you when she gave you a tour upon your first arrival.

Amy Rosalie— the woman who ran the Post Office looked up from a book upon hearing the door open, and smiled widely at you.

She was one of the oldest women here, say of course, from Harper. She was grey-haired and looked as if she had been around when the building she sat in was first made— though she remembered clearly when the original buildings had been blown up sometime during her infancy. She had slight sight issues, and had to use the chunkiest glasses you had ever seen— black-rimmed and rectangular, which seemed to make her eyes five times bigger.

Though her eyes were failing, her ears were more sharp than most. If something happened between or to anyone on the island, she would miraculously know about it— her favourite hobby seemed to be gossip.

"Just the person I was hoping to see!" She declared happily, standing up on her frail legs and hobbling to the filing cabinets behind her. "You've got very important mail, the two of you."

Russia looked down at you— you looked right back, a strange look held between your eyes.

"From who?" You asked as she pulled a small white envelope out and wobbled back to the counter. You quickly stepped up to take it from her so she could sit down again, tucking the loaf of bread under your arm. "Read it and find out." She smiled, watching as you stared down at it, Russia leaning over your shoulder.

The building was poorly lit, the old musty windows let very little light in, it was hard to even see the envelope, never mind the small lettering of the sender.

You thanked her for giving it to you and backed back out, wanting to bring it into the light of the Sun so you could read it better.

Russia followed after you— he seemed a little more skittish now. Glancing up and around constantly, as if he didn't know where he was all of a sudden.

Under the light from above you could finally see who it was from. In beautiful calligraphy— almost as if it was printed, the sender had written your name and address in the centre, while their name, United Nations, was written in the top left.

"Oh hey, it's from UN, want to read it with me?" You chirped as you looked up at the country with a smile.

But that didn't last long.

He had gone completely pale, the colours of his flag draining from his face— his tired white eyes wide and unmoving, chest heaving and falling in quick succession.

He looked just as he had this morning.

You had spent hours holding him. Listening to him diligently as he sobbed all the while— he promised you he had felt better after he said it all. How he felt like he was never enough, that he hated himself, how life just didn't seem worth living, but there was no way he could escape it from his immortal body.

That he was scared he would be miserable forever.

He had promised you he would improve, that he wouldn't be so scared to let himself be happy.

But it just wasn't that easy. He stood, frozen like a deer in headlights before you, that same look of utter defeat upon his face.

"Don't open zat." He mumbled— low and hesitant, eyes never blinking, his mind racing yet empty all at once. "Why not?" You asked, stepping closer to him in case he wanted to say something only you should hear.

But he only lost more of his breath, his face going paler, the horror he had set in stone as he swayed on his feet. He couldn't answer— he couldn't bring himself to tell you that he was scared it was something he didn't want to hear.

He hated to admit it, but UN was completely right. This kind of quiet scheduled life was doing him good— you were doing him some good. The comfort you gave him was unmatched, like the Moon's light in the twilight, you guided him through a plane of wooded depths and brought him home.

He was scared all this would be taken away from him. That the UN would say his time here was up, and he would be forced back into that tiny wooden cabin in the icy tundra of his home. Surrounded by nothing but memories of who he was, the life that had been forced onto him.

He couldn't take any more of that life, not when he was only just discovering that wasn't the only way to live.

Russia turned away— walking right past you, beginning back towards the lighthouse.

Maybe all he needed was a drink to calm his nerves, then he could open it.

"Where are you going? Come on it's nothing bad, I'm sure." You called after him as you jogged to catch up. But Russia stopped dead at your words, turning back to face you.

You never pictured you would feel scared when you stood before him.

"I don't fucking kare what it is (□/□), open it by yourself, or are you too fucking useless to do anything by yourself?" He snapped, glaring down at you, those sad eyes replaced by something else— but you knew it wasn't anger.

It was full, blown, terror.

"Russia please—" You began, but he wouldn't let you finish. "Just fuck off, you're adult, do it by yourself." He spat, then turned, and left you there— completely dumbfounded.

You watched him go for a moment, back towards your shared home, then glanced down at the letter.

It couldn't be bad, could it?

H   C

C HAPTER 16

You tore open the envelope with shaking hands. Your apprehension undeniable.

You had waited so long for this letter, this small rectangular paper that seemed so insignificant on its surface. But held your future within it.

You pulled the letter out slowly— painstakingly. Your heart roaring in your chest, eyes wide and expectant. Blood rushing through every inch of your body, as if it was trying its hardest to calm the storm brewing in your chest.

You read the words cautiously.

Skimming over the technical words— the thank yous for applying and whatnot. And looked for the treasured words of, 'You're hired!'

"Well, what does it say? Stop edging me, did you get the fucking job or not?" Your best friend bellowed from his place on the bed— tucked neatly under the white covers, his arms folded.

"Would you shut up for two seconds, I'm reading." You mumbled, gripping the sheet harder as you pulled it closer to you. The longer you stared, the more you found it harder to read— as if the dread of being denied was blurring your eyes. Blocking you from seeing anything, from reading what you desperately needed to hear.

He grumbled, copying your words in a high-pitched mocking tone, flapping his fingers in a fake mouth. You rolled your eyes, and probed further.

Then you saw it— right at the bottom of the page, buried under all the irrelevant words above it.

'We're more than happy to welcome you to Ivymallow as our new, round-the-clock, lighthouse keeper!'

You couldn't believe it. After searching so long for a job, reviewing all your options in life over and over and over again— searching in vain for something that could release you from the entrenched rat race of an average life.

You finally found it.

You threw your arms up and jumped with joy— hopping up to embrace your friend in an open-arm hug that you still felt even to this day— when you missed that moment in time.

"Hell yeah (□/□)! I'm so proud of you!" He laughed as you almost sobbed into his chest, your joy choking you in that moment. Your excitement contagious and uncontainable.

"You'll visit me when I get settled in, won't you?" You had asked him then, hopeful in the moment.

You were so caught up in your exhilaration you didn't want it to end. You didn't want to think you would have no one to share it with. He was right there— he watched you open the letter of acceptance and saw how happy it made you.

"I promise."

He had said.

Lying in his hospital bed.

You never imagined you would have to say goodbye before you even moved away. He would never get the chance to come visit you.

Your life had just begun, but his, as it seemed, was ready to end.

You left him behind.

The letter snug in your pocket— an umbrella above your head as you listened to the priest's eulogy in the rain. You refused to look at his gravestone that day. Concentrating instead on the feeling of the paper boat tickets in your other pocket. Holding onto them for some kind of comfort.

You left the next day, it seemed cruel to leave him behind like that, but in the moment that's all you wanted to do. To run from it all. The loss you felt was monumental— you felt nothing at all when you finally arrived and saw where you were going to live.

But that was so long ago now, wasn't it?

He would be happy for you, you just knew he would.

As you stepped through the door of the local creamers years later. Needing to pick up some fresh butter and milk. Life was ordinary now, you didn't like to think about him often.

"Hello (□/□), how are you today?" Josh Harriet asked as you walked through, ringing the little overhead bell. "I'm okay, and you?"

Josh smiled, halting his past work of counting money from the till to turn his attention onto you. "I'm good thank you."

The letter from the UN was still between your fingers, he seemed to notice it as you walked closer— but if he did, he didn't mention it, rather he moved onto business almost immediately. "The usual stuff is it?" He asked as he stepped out from behind the counter, going to one of the cold boxes, and pulling a slab of butter dressed in grease paper, then pulling a carton of milk alongside it. "Sure is." You replied, leaning against the till.

You dug through your pockets to retrieve some cash, but you stopped before you could.

Josh placed your items on the counter, giving you a weird look as you stood nearly frozen to the spot. "Say," you began, turning oddly on your heels to face him, tossing your bread onto the counter so you could lean on it, "Can you do me a favour and open this with me? It's from the United Nations."

Josh's brows lifted instantly, his intrigue spiking as soon as you said the letters sender out loud. He leant his body over the counter, elbows pressed down to get a better look at the envelope you held out. "Of course I will, why do you ask though?"

You thought about it.

You were never too keen on opening letters alone, you found yourself always repeating the past when it came to that. If there was one thing you learned, it's that it's easier to accept change when there's someone there with you.

"Well, I picked it up earlier, and Russia was there with me right?" You explained, drawing an interested 'right' from Josh. "But when he saw it he got mad at me, like I did something, and stormed off in a fit." You finished, raising your arms and letting them fall melodramatically.

Josh nodded his head, turning to face downward as he thought. Cupping his hands together all the while. "I wouldn't worry about it too much, I'd say he's just worried about getting taken back." He assured you, meeting your eyes with an acquisitive look, "Surely living here is better than the fast life he used to live, he's probably just a bit scared."

You blew a breath out, a few strands of hair becoming entangled and blowing upward. "I suppose you're right." You mumbled, gazing back down at the letter. Running your thumb over the print of your name. It was funny how he addressed it to you— not Russia. Perhaps it wasn't about him at all, perhaps UN just wished to see how you were.

But you knew that wouldn't make any sense. Russia saw it too when you showed it to him. You had to stop yourself from sighing again.

"You really care about him, don't you?" Josh suddenly spoke from beside you, a soft smile across his face when you met his gaze. "Of course I do, he's my guest." You replied rather snappy— knowing what he was trying to get out with that smile of his.

But your tone only made him laugh and stand back straight. His eyebrows wiggled mockingly as he spoke. "I think someone's got a little crush."

You slapped your hands down on the counter, making Josh laugh louder as he backed away a little. "No, I don't, you can shut up!" You yelled, though you couldn't hold it for long— as you burst out into laughter as well. Turning your head as you did so, double-checking that no one heard your sudden outburst.

You did care for him, of course, you cared for him. But you didn't think it was like that. You cared only cause you needed to— if there was anything that strange man needed now, was someone to listen to him. You knew that better than he himself did.

What you had was platonic, wasn't it?

"Go on then, open it, I'm curious now." Josh gestured toward the envelope, opting you to flip it over and tear the seams. Placing the discarded envelope on the till, which Josh took in hand and glanced over.

The letter was just what you thought it was.

A question of how Russia was fairing. If he had settled well or not— and requesting a reply back to the given address when able.

You read it aloud for the dairy farmer to hear. Who listened diligently with squinted eyes. His hands cupped in front of his lips, brows furrowed.

When you finished you met his eyes, there was a moment of silence before he hummed and stood upright again. "You should read it to Russia, he needs to hear it."

You turned back to the paper between your fingers.

On the inside, it was addressed to the both of you— but written with you in mind. Asking how he was from your perspective, rather than his.

You thought for a moment how he could find that a little disparaging, but in the end, you had to accept that it was a friendly thing. Perhaps he knew Russia would hate to find a letter addressed to him from the man who sent him here.

"I don't know if he'd want to hear it." You relied, creasing the corners of the egg-white paper with your thumbs. "Then wait until evening once he's calmed down." Josh reasoned— ever the mature voice in a room.

You would have agreed, nodding your head and promising you'd wait. But there was this thought you had— fleeting and rudimentary. An idea that made much more sense the longer you thought of it— a conceived fear that spoke volumes amongst the ebb and flow of your thoughts.

Even after letting him reach out and acknowledge what he was doing to himself. That didn't mean he'd automatically be cured. As if the struggles he lived with would just vanish because he talked about them once.

You realised then that you left him, alone, when he very clearly had some form of a breakdown.

Your blood went cold.

To see someone else— attached by a ribbon, eye to eye now unreachable— the gradation of arm's length told by the ending of time, and the continuation of the Earth's spin now with one less burden.

You snatched the envelope back and slid the letter back in, backing up as you fiddled with the paper. "I have to go." You mumbled to Josh, fluidly spilling your words— beginning to sprint for the door and towards your lighthouse. Hoping you'd find him well.

"It was nice seeing you, good luck!" Josh called as you flung the door open and threw yourself out— completely missing how Josh yelled from his store that you forgot your items.

Your feet beat against the ground, the wind whipped at your hair as you flung your body as fast as you could. People stopped and watched you weirdly but you didn't care.

Your lighthouse taunted you from across the island, its high-rising walls of red and white sticking up from the cliffs like a candy cane— directing you to its doors where you were terrified to find something familiar, yet all the more painful.

It always troubled you on why she did it. She didn't leave a note, she didn't see anyone that night— but she did call. Only, you had been busy drinking— you were too inebriated to pick up the phone. You sent her right to voicemail. You had been her sought-out hotline, her last ditch effort to save herself.

Now she would never call you again.

You would never truly know why she did it.

But it was no one's fault but yours.

You would never forget that.

As you ran down the dirt path towards your home, letter flapping in the wind, legs kicking exhaustedly at the mud— you were afraid it would be like that again.

Did he not believe you when you said you would always be there?

Perhaps, he was right.

This was your second missed call.

G sO A sL

C HAPTER 17

You banged on the door— each in quick succession, your lungs screaming aloud, the fear and panic impassible, your desperation insurmountable.

You cried and cried for your mother to open the door— to let you in and out of the pitch-black hallway, your own screaming scaring you, the lack of breath from your crying making you feel as though you were dying. Slowly drowning in the darkness around you as you threw your fists into the door over and over and over again.

You screamed aloud for your mother louder and louder each time— all you wanted was to be let in, you had a nightmare and wished to sleep with her.

To be protected in your young age by your loving mother.

There was a gargling and choking sound emanating from somewhere— you couldn't tell where, you were too scared to even register your own voice, the screaming your throat let out only frightening you more.

To your young mind, it sounded as though something was in the hallway with you— drawing closer and closer with each screech you let out, opening its jaws in the darkness and grinding its teeth just above your head as you crumpled on the ground— still crying for your mother to save you.

You banged on the door harder, the gargling getting louder— the spluttering and vomiting gaining in speed and volume, coating your ears as you bellowed into the sound of what you imagined to be your death. Stalking you down the hall.

You reached up with your fingers, grasping the doorknob and turning— the gurgling ceased, your crying quelled, you stared through the door into the room with wide eyes— parting your lips to scream once more, eyes wide and watering, throat croaking and dry, you caterwauled into the empty air—

"Russia!"

You ran upstairs as fast as you could, jumping two steps at a time, tripping over your legs. You had tried to make it across the island in seconds flat but the ground was uneven and the journey long. You had tumbled and wasted time cautiously dodging mud mounds and holes, knowing all the while you had left Russia alone with his thoughts and tendencies.

But now you had made it, panting and exhausted, sweat dripping from your forehead, your legs aching, muscles on fire.

You found him right where you thought you would— where you always used to find him. Back before he gave himself some kind of false hope.

His back was against the kitchen table, his legs sprawled out in front of him, a bottle in his hands— head low and unresponsive, clearly drunk.

"Russia..." You breathlessly called, leaning against the railing to catch your breath. "It's not what you think it is, he was only asking how you are."

Russia gurgled from where he sat, mumbling incoherently to himself, his head moving oddly as he brought it up to look at you. His eyes sagging, the world undoubtedly spinning for him. He didn't even seem as though he could see you. Yet you walked toward him anyway, standing just above him.

"I'm sorry," he mumbled, ragged through his intoxication, his body moving in stiff sudden jolts that shook him. "I know you zink I'm better zan zis."

You sat down in front of him— he seemed to have given up at meeting your gaze through his cloud of inebriation. Everything was the same to him— his mind in a different place entirely. The only thing that was real to him in that moment was nothing.

He was too intoxicated to think at all.

There was nothing to think about, there was nothing to touch or feel, you before him seemed a million miles away— there was just nothing.

No matter how he tried to convince himself that this was a moment he was living, eventually, he would slip away again— his mind was just not there.

Time flew in circles, everything parted while the sky fell— something was there, he knew it was, but there was just nothing at all.

He could hardly hear you as you spoke.

"You don't have to feel bad, it's okay, I'll read it to you when you're feeling up for it."

You drew closer to him and took the bottle from his limp hands, he didn't protest nor try to take it back. He merely gurgled again, hiccuping in between the little noises he let out. Before he gathered his words in a slurred and sluggish way. "I was skared. I vas so skared zis life vould be taken avay from me."

You settled further against the floor, sitting with your knees to your chest, arms wrapped around them. "It's okay, it doesn't matter all that much, what happens, will happen."

But Russia shook his head, bringing his knee up, a hand across his face, his shoulders beginning to shake. "It does." He cried, suddenly getting loud as his slurred voice crumbled. The world in fractured seconds to him, spinning as he lay still, his shame unavoidable.

"It doesn't, nothing matters, you don't have to worry at all." You muttered, trying what you could to comfort him. But you were finding it difficult. This time you weren't speaking to someone who could hear you. You were speaking to a man who was lost between this world and the next— drowned in a bottle he set upon himself.

"It matters to me." He fumbled through his falling spirit. The pure empty oblivion he felt in the morning back completely— devouring his soul with its sharp teeth that begged him to drink more, so he could pass out for hours and no longer have to be a part of a world he couldn't stand— at least for a while.

"Why?" You asked, letting your legs fall a little, the grip you had waning.

Russia's hand fell, his eyes finally reaching up to meet yours. They were red and puffy, and it was clear he had been crying again, the glimmer of tears shining in your eyes, bubbling and twinkling like stars.

He opened his lips to speak, his eyes widening as he seemed to realise what he was about to say, his head bobbing and swaying. "I love you."

You felt your heart drop.

Before it hit something hard in your chest— and shattered into a million pieces.

"What do you mean?"

Russia noticed how your expression changed, but wasn't in the right state of mind to understand why.

But you knew. You had loved so many people in your life, and every single one of them, was gone now. Buried in the past, or in graves of their own.

You promised yourself you would never love another person. You couldn't take any more heartbreak.

Yet, here he was, saying those words you so hated. He was only temporary in your life— you knew that. He was as transient as the Sun in the morning and the Moon at the dead of night.

He would leave your life just as everyone else had.

You couldn't allow him to take another piece of your soul with him. There wasn't much left to take.

"I mean zat I love you." He reiterated, staring at you still with those eyes— an odd clarity in them, juxtaposed to the ebb and flow of his body and slur of his voice.

"I vant to tell you how much you mean to me, I vant to spend every moment I have here vith you, I vant to make you feel like the only voman in the vorld, I vant to spoil you rotten. I vant— you."

You could do nothing more than stare.

And he stared right back.

Clarity was between his gaze— perfect realisation of something he didn't know before. Acceptance in his mind, somehow knowing more now he was inebriated, than when he was sober.

But you were his complete opposite. Your intention was never to make him feel this way— your biggest fear was loving someone. After all the people you had to bury, you were scared of having to do it again— metaphorically or not.

Each time you said goodbye to someone, you left a little of your soul at their gravestone. You had so little left to give. You were scared now, that he was being honest, because you knew, if you gave what he wanted back, there would be nothing left of you once he returned to his old life.

You didn't want him to think of you like that— you didn't want to think of him like that. But part of you knew, there was no getting away from it.

"You're drunk, you don't know what you're saying, this isn't funny."

You drew yourself away from him. Pushing back against the ground. Dragging yourself away, putting more distance between the two of you.

Russia's gaze turned desperate. He drunkenly leaned forward, his body swaying— eyes flickering as he lost that clarity a little, tears swelling again.

"But I do," He mumbled, begging you to accept it, to release the denial you had placed yourself under and let loose, handing yourself to him— so the two of you could finally find some happiness. "I love zat you dart your eyes around when you're nervous, I love zat you don't blow smoke out your mouth, you just let it all puff out like cloud, I love zat you smooth your clothes out when you're vorried about how you look, I love zat you sigh whenever you sit down, I love zat you valk with your hands intertvined when you have nowhere else to put zem, I love zat you crinkle your nose when you drink alkohol."

His tears dried by themselves— he seemed to have convinced himself something. His perfect clarity back, an epiphany amongst the blur of intoxication. "I love you, (□/□). I love you."

All you could do was shake your head. Your soul burning within your body, blood on fire and skin crawling with the knowledge that you were about to lose someone else.

You had spent so long being scared— it was your only reaction now. It was the only thing you really knew, a trust fall you relayed your life to. Allowing it to take you every time. Engulfing whatever there was left of you. Heart and soul entrapped in the same glass case, locked— key thrown to the waves.

You stood slowly to your feet. His eyes followed you, tears building, his hope dissipated— clarity fading, he was just as scared as you were.

"No. No, you don't, this joke you're playing isn't funny Russia, you're drunk, get yourself a drink of water and sober up." You spat. Then turned to head upstairs.

You expected him to call for you, to say something more— something that would give him release, but burning despair for you.

But there was nothing more— all you could hear now, was the sound of sobbing.

In an attempt to help yourself, all you did was break someone else.

In the end, it seems, you did lie, you wouldn't always be there for him.

Not when he needed you the most.

D   As

C HAPTER 18

Russia's eyes blinked open— groggily.

His mind pounding in his skull. Muscles weak and inflamed as he pushed himself up, groaning and holding his head.

He wasn't in his bed. He had fallen asleep on the floor of the kitchen. His body freezing in the open air— arms and back aching from having slept on the hard ground.

He couldn't remember why he was there. He couldn't remember how he got there.

Everything seemed a million miles away as he pushed himself to his feet— a copy of a copy of a copy, a repented image relaying an incomplete story, halfway finished, halfway began.

He couldn't remember anything of what had happened. Of why he had slept on the floor— his stomach began to burn. Twisting and cramping, rumbling as it squeezed, sickening him to some great extent.

He cupped his mouth with a fist— his other arm around his stomach, and ran. Down the winding stairs, down each floor, down to the door and out into the world beyond.

His muscles cramped, his head reeled— heart beating wildly in his ribcage, punching desperately at the walls, cracking and shattering the breath in his chest.

He rushed through the grass— feeling a sickening liquid crawl up his throat. Chunky and bitter, sharp in taste, staining his throat as slabs of old half-digested food clogged his oesophagus.

He threw the outhouse door open— dropping to his knees he began harking up his insides into the toilet. Finding a disgusting grip on whatever was available, the flaps of his hat dangling toward the water— gagging rolled his eyes back, constant spasms of his throat shook his body and forced him to vomit more.

There was nothing he could do to help himself.

He hardly noticed when you came in. Awoken by his sudden springing, following to find him vomiting alone.

You stepped up behind him, dropping to your knees also and taking his hat from him. Resting it on your lap.

You rubbed his back as he finished, pulling his head back up and attempting to wipe his lips— though before he could, you grabbed his wrist and moved his hand away, wiping them yourself with a clean bit of toilet paper— much to Russia's surprise.

But he was too ill to do anything else. To say something more. He merely leaned against the toilet bowl, his head bowed— eyes closed, waiting to see if that sickening feeling would crawl back up again.

"How are you feeling?" You asked, shuffling to get comfy. Before you handed his hat back out for him to take. "Like shit." He mumbled. "What happened last night?"

You looked away. He was trying to fix his hat on his head— shuffling it constantly. Seated just inches in front of you, folded knee brushing yours, the afterglow of whatever breath he had bushing against you.

You hadn't forgotten last night.

It was one of the worst you ever had.

For hours— you were forced to listen to the sound of him crying, on repeat. For hours, he sobbed, sniffling all the while. Whilst you laid in bed, eyes to the ceiling, covers to your chin, listening— and wanting to do the sam e.

You didn't want to explain that to him. So you chose to remain silent. Rather, standing back to your feet— Russia keeping his eyes on yours all the while, before you turned to leave.

You didn't want to relive yesterday.

You didn't want him to remember what you had done to him.

Though before you could, he grabbed your wrist, drawing his torso a little higher. Hope ablaze in those sad heavy eyes. "Do you vant to go somewhere vith me? I'd really like to see rest of island."

You took the time to stare into the white plane of pooled Earth that lay behind the glass of his eye. Soft and subtle— drizzling within, lonely and isolated, always to see in pairs— but never to see its pair.

"I don't really feel like it today." You mumbled, turning away, pulling your arm tenderly, hoping he'd let go. But he didn't. He gazed up at you with those pooled eyes— Moon's reflection bathing within, rippling and suckling— a testament to his all-reverent seclusion. "Is something wrong? Did I say something?"

You couldn't look away. Those eyes— hurt and severed, a crystallise engulfing the light around it, a blackhole expelling all the joy from his soul— not a sense of shine in his sclera, only empty agony. The weight of sorrow, jaws of despair, each a finger coiled, a day in the life for him— you could see that clear. But how horrible you felt for him now.

How horrible it felt knowing you were pushing him under the waves— just to hold your head above the water.

"What do you think of me?" You asked, slowly. He released your wrist, hesitant as he recoiled his hand back to himself— shuffling to move away from the toilet more.

"I zink you're delightful." He stated— matter-of-factly, his eyes hardening, as if he believed you to feel self-loathing in the moment, and wanted to deny it.

"Do you think you love me?"

He went red, completely. Crimson blush patted under his eyes, those sunken lids inflamed, the windows of his soul stretched wide— his lips taut as he reviewed your words over and over in his mind. All the while having to bear the uncomfortable softness of your gaze.

"Is zat what I said last night?" He asked carefully, as if he imagined himself to be walking on thin ice— only, that was all in his mind. A made-up anxiety his head introduced to quell the panic in his indecisiveness.

You nodded your head.

His anxiety spiked tenfold. Pouring through his veins like pressurised magma— his heart unresponsive as it wracked against itself, he heard it everywhere but within him. He felt his blood in his head, pooling in his temples, a kind of gripping headache nuzzling into his psyche.

"I'm really sorry (□/□), I vas drunk, I didn't mean to say zat. I meant no harm, really I didn't." He gushed, shaking his hands in front of him— his face redder by the second, tense and immovable, hunched into himself.

But you didn't say anything more.

Your eyes were to the ground, you no longer wished to put yourself through the anguish of having to meet his pained eyes. You couldn't do that to yourself. All you wanted was for this to vanish— was for him to take it back, and forget he ever felt anything for you.

But he didn't like the look on your face.

If his eyes had expressions, it would be what you showed, on display for all to see, the big screen showing. "I vas telling truth," He began, mumbling it all, trying what he could to get you to meet his eye again. To acknowledge him in some other way.

But he never got to finish.

"Tell me it's not true. Tell me you're lying. Please, it's all I need to hear."

Russia drew a breath in. You still didn't look his way. Your eyes were on the floor, that's where they seemed to be staying— cold and unresponsive, sorrow behind taciturn. "Of kourse I mean it—"

But you didn't let him finish. Whatever he wanted to say, would never be said. You didn't want to hear what came next— you couldn't bring yourself to listen.

"I can't do this." You muttered, turning your back on him, beginning to walk towards the door— heels dragging.

"(□/□), please," Russia called, sitting more upright, hoisting himself in the hopes you would turn around and face him again.

He didn't care for what reason. You could have turned to yell at him. To curse him out. To threaten and belittle him. To run him out of your home.

No matter what it was, he would have been happier.

Even if you turned to hate him, he would be happy you turned back for him at all.

"I have to write back to UN."

But you never turned to face him. His soul crushed as you opened the door.

And left him where he lay.

Russia breathed a breath in, then two, then three.

Soon he was gasping.

A hand at his chest, the other gripping the toilet bowl, he felt two seconds from dry heaving until he spewed blood all over the floor. Try as he might, there was no more breath for him to breathe— his lungs were empty, his head full to bursting, a balloon strung up too tight.

He had been wrong, of course, he had been wrong. When was he ever right?

He gasped desperately— hyperventilating into his hand, coughing over himself, chest wheezing in and out in and out— constantly, begging for some air he couldn't find.

Why, he needn't have it! What he thought he needed before was all in his mind. Who would care if he couldn't breathe any longer? Certainly not you.

And in turn, as a favour of his proclaimed love.

He wouldn't care about you either.

He didn't, care about you.

It was all a lie to himself. You were the first woman who gave him any proper attention, of course, he was going to think he liked you.

But that wasn't true, it couldn't be.

May the Stars despise the Sun— such a radiant deity christening a world of blue, man and beast may gaze up at the eye of the beholder, shaken by the blinding luminosity barren in their eyes. A powerful dissident peeling the clouds back, a bringer of life in the dead of Winter and the thief of nurture in the Summer.

Yet the Stars, hopeless and meaningless— a show pony to the couplet of the Moon— the bride of their combatant. The love story of the night, worthless to the sky, the Earth, too far away to hold the world in constant duty. A bystander in the spilt pale of the milky cloak.

You struck admiration wherever you went.

He never even made the game.

He envied you. He despised you.He judged you. He deplored you.

He didn't love you. You didn't love him.

There was an understanding between the two of you. A hatred for themselves, and the other— falsely.

You meant nothing to him. He meant nothing to you.

You were worthless, as was he.

He lowered his head, and fought himself to hold his tears.

The two of you were so different— yet the exact same.